The Sheriff's Second Chance

Michelle Celmer

HARLEQUIN® SPECIAL EDITION®

Recycling programs
for this product may
not exist in your area.

ISBN-13: 978-0-373-65790-2

THE SHERIFF'S SECOND CHANCE

HARLEQUIN®

Printed in U.S.A.

™ www.Harlequin.com

MICHELLE CELMER

is a bestselling author of more than thirty books. When she's not writing, she likes to spend time with her husband, kids, grandchildren and a menagerie of animals.

Michelle loves to hear from readers. Visit her website, www.michellecelmer.com, like her on Facebook or write her at P.O. Box 300, Clawson, MI 48017.

For my Mom,
who never once doubted that I would be a success

For my Dad,
who continues to support and encourage me

For Charles,
who is not just a kick-ass editor, but a friend

For Melissa,
whose faith in me has driven my career
since she bought my first book

For my children and grandchildren,
who never fail to remind me of what's important

And finally, for Steve,
whose strength has taught me that
giving up is never an option

Chapter One

The instant Deputy Sheriff Nathan Jefferies pulled his cruiser into the diner lot and saw his dad, P.J., standing out front instead of waiting inside like he always did, he knew something was up. He grabbed the phone he'd lobbed onto the dash when he'd walked Cody into day care, and, sure enough, there were two missed calls from his dad and two more from his mom.

By the time he killed the engine and climbed out of the car, his dad was standing at the driver's side door—definitely not their usual routine. "Something wrong?"

The old man shrugged. "I just thought maybe we could try someplace different for a change."

Someplace different? Was his dad forgetting where they lived? With a population of 1,633, Paradise, Colorado, didn't exactly have a huge selection when it came to dining establishments. There was Joe's Place, but that didn't open until lunch, and there was Lou's Diner. Aside from those, and the Howard Johnson's on the highway several miles east of town, there wasn't anywhere else within twenty miles to get a decent breakfast. Or any breakfast for that matter.

Something was definitely up. "What's going on, Dad?"

His dad sighed and rubbed a hand across a jawline beginning to sag with age. "Son, she's back."

Nate wasn't sure what was more pathetic: that he knew exactly who "she" was, or that he still gave a damn after all these years.

He steeled himself against the residual sting of rejection, the burn of betrayal that still seared his heart like acid.

"Was bound to happen eventually, I s'pose," his dad said. "She couldn't stay away forever."

Not forever. Just seven years.

Seven years with no explanation of why, after two years together, she'd packed her bags and left town. Nothing but that pathetic excuse for an apology she'd sent him weeks later.

Dear Nate, I'm so, so sorry...

Nate shook away the memory.

"We could skip breakfast today, son. We don't have to go in there."

Nate blinked. "She's *here,* at the diner?"

His dad nodded.

Everyone in the restaurant had seen him pull up. He had no choice but to go in. And it wasn't just a matter of his pride, although that was part of it. As a deputy sheriff, he had a reputation to uphold. If people began to see him as a coward, his credibility as peacekeeper in town would be compromised. And what could be more cowardly than turning tail and running from an estranged girlfriend seven years after the breakup?

"Let's go." He marched up the walk and shouldered his way through the door. The second his shoe hit the black-and-white-checked linoleum floor, twenty or so pairs of eyes snapped in his direction and bore into him like an auger biting through steel. In a town the size of Paradise, where everyone's nose was in everyone else's business, good news traveled fast.

And bad news traveled even faster.

This reunion would be stressful enough without an audience, but it was too late to turn back now. A swift survey of the interior revealed many familiar and curious faces, but not the one he was anticipating. And dreading.

The short walk to the counter felt like a mile. He slid onto his usual stool beside George Simmons, owner of Simmons Hardware, and his dad sat beside him.

"Mornin', Deputy," George said, then nodded to Nate's dad. "Mornin', P.J."

"Mornin', George," P.J. returned. "How are things down at the hardware store?"

George shrugged. "Can't complain. How's the house coming along?" he asked, referring to the Victorian-era home Nate's parents had been renovating.

"It's comin'."

"Got that tile laid in the downstairs bathroom?"

P.J. nodded. "Just about."

They had a similar conversation every morning, yet today it felt stilted and awkward. To add to the tension, Nate could feel the gaze of the entire restaurant pinned against his back.

Their waitress, Delores Freeburg, who had worked at the diner as long as Nate could remember, appeared with a decanter of coffee and poured them each a cup. "Morning, Nate, P.J. Will you have the usual?"

"Just coffee for me," Nate said. His belly was too tied in knots to choke down eggs and bacon.

P.J. patted the paunch that had begun to creep over his belt and said, "I'm starving. The usual for me."

Delores winked and left to put in the order, but not before shooting Nate a glance rife with curiosity.

There was a brief, awkward silence, then George said, "So, Nate, I guess you've heard the news."

"I heard." And he didn't care to talk about it.

"Been a long time," George persisted.

Nate poured cream and sugar in his cup. The idea of drinking it made his stomach turn, but he forced himself to take a sip, burning the hell out of his tongue in the process.

"Seven years," his dad answered for him, and Nate shot him a look that said, *Don't encourage him.*

But George needed no encouragement. He was a worse gossip than most of the women at Shear Genius, the salon Nate's ex-wife owned.

Nate pulled out his phone and pretended to check his messages, but that didn't stop George.

"Guess she got herself into a fix up there in New York." George shook his head, as though he could relate, even though he'd never lived a day outside of their small town. "Some sort of federal investigation into her financial firm."

"I hope you also heard that I'm not personally

under any suspicion," a female voice stated from be-hind them. A voice that after seven years was still so familiar, Nate's heart climbed up his throat and lodged there. Caitlyn Cavanaugh walked around the counter, facing them now, but Nate kept his eyes on his phone screen.

"Welcome back, Caitie," his dad said.

"Hi, P.J. Long time no see."

"When did you get home?"

"Just last night."

"And your parents have you back to work *already?*"

"I offered. Deb called in sick. But I'll warn you, I may be a bit rusty. I haven't waited tables in almost five years."

"Well," P.J. said with a shrug. "You know that noth-ing much ever changes around here."

"I guess not."

Nate could feel her eyes on him, but he couldn't make himself lift his gaze. Maybe if he ignored her, it wouldn't be real.

"Hello, Nate," she said, her voice quiet.

He had no choice but to look at her now, and when he lifted his head and his eyes snagged on hers, every bit of pain and rejection he'd felt when she left slammed him in the gut like a fist.

In her waitress uniform she looked almost exactly the same. A little older, maybe, her pale blond hair lon-ger than the shoulder-length, no-nonsense style she'd worn in high school. And her smile wasn't quite as carefree. But she was still his Caitie—

No, she wasn't *his* anything.

Underneath the pain, the anger still simmered. It

threatened to boil over and spill out like molten lava onto the Formica countertop.

He said the only thing he could, so she would understand exactly where she stood. "That's Deputy Sheriff to you, Miss Cavanaugh."

So that was the way it was going to be?

Caitlyn Cavanaugh wasn't really surprised. Of course she had hoped that after all these years Nate would have forgiven her, or at the very least, let go of the animosity.

Apparently not. And that was not at all like the Nate she used to know. That Nate was so laid-back, so easygoing and nonconfrontational. After two years together she could count on one hand how many times they had argued. Come to think of it, she'd never seen him really *angry* at anyone.

Until now.

Under the icy exterior, he was seething. And though she would never admit it to another living soul, after all these years, it stung. Badly. But she refused to be labeled the only bad guy when he was just as guilty of betrayal. She may have left town, and she wouldn't deny that sending a vague letter in lieu of a real explanation was a cowardly thing to do. But he seemed to be forgetting that he married her *best friend* only *three months* after she left.

If it killed her, she would never let him know just how much that had hurt.

"I beg your pardon, Deputy," she said, pasting on a polite yet vaguely disinterested smile. One he didn't return, not that she had expected him to. He'd always had a sweet, slightly lopsided grin that never failed to melt her on the spot. And hadn't that been one of their biggest problems? She never could tell him no.

Thank goodness her dad, Lou, who was manning the grill, chose that instant to call an order up, putting an end to what would only become an increasingly awkward conversation.

"Enjoy your breakfast, gentleman," she said, then turned and crossed to the order window to grab the plates. Her dad peered at her from the other side. Concern crinkled the corners of his eyes. Kind eyes, her mom liked to say.

"You okay?" he asked.

"Fine," she said, even though she was anything but.

"You don't look fine. Why don't you take a break? Delores can cover your tables for a few minutes."

As much as she wanted to escape, at least until Nate finished his coffee and left, that wasn't even an option. If she could handle high-profile clients with multimillion-dollar portfolios, she could handle a snarky ex-boyfriend. And if she couldn't...well, she would never give him the satisfaction of knowing how much seeing him had rattled her. Besides, if they were going to live in the same town together, even if it was only temporary, she would just have to get used to running into him every now and then.

"I'm okay, Dad."

He didn't look as though he believed her, but he didn't push the issue.

She grabbed the plates and turned, slamming into Delores, who was standing at the juice machine. The glass she was filling slipped from her hand and crashed to the floor, shattering into a million pieces.

"Oh, Delores! I'm so sorry," Caitie said, her cheeks

burning with embarrassment. She didn't have to turn to know that everyone was staring at her. She could feel it.

Could this morning get any worse? Any more humiliating?

"It's okay, hon," Delores said, patting her arm.

"I'll clean it up."

"You take care of your order. I'll get it."

"Are you sure?"

Delores nodded and said softly, "Just take a deep breath and try to relax, hon. It'll get easier, I promise."

A divorcée five times over, Delores was pretty much the town authority on failed relationships, and Caitie knew she was right. This was just harder than she thought it would be. The feelings she'd buried a long time ago were fighting their way up to the surface.

Avoiding the counter—and Nate—Caitie delivered her order to the customers in the back corner, then stopped at the booth beside it whose occupants had just been seated. She knew Lindy and Zoey from high school, and though they'd been a grade ahead of Caitie, they had all been on the cheerleading squad together.

There was a third woman with them Caitie didn't recognize. It was obvious by their sudden silence as she approached the table that they had been talking about her. No doubt Lindy and Zoey were telling their friend the tale of Cait's defection from her hometown.

What a stellar first day back this had turned out to be and it was barely 9:00 a.m.

Caitie raised her chin a notch and smiled. "Hello, Lindy, Zoey. Long time no see."

"That's bound to happen when you leave town without a word," Lindy said, her eyes cold.

Making a clean break had been her only option. She didn't expect Lindy or anyone else to understand that.

At least Caitie had escaped the grips of their small town. She had followed her dream and for a while had been a success—and would be again just as soon as she found a new job. This trip home was a temporary diversion. She hoped.

"Word is you had some trouble," Zoey added. "I'm sorry things didn't work out."

Caitie kept the smile firmly in place. Most people would consider going off to college, landing a cushy job at a prestigious finance firm and making a life for herself in New York an impressive feat. Zoey, on the other hand, seemed to revel in her failure. "I'm here temporarily. I'm going back to New York as soon as I find a new job."

"We should all get together for drinks and catch up," Zoey said, with a plastic, artificially whitened smile. She and Caitie had never been what anyone would call close friends. And from the looks of her styled hair, manicured nails and designer clothes, her wealthy father was still spoiling her rotten.

"That sounds like fun," Caitie said, knowing she would do no such thing. It would be a fishing expedition for gossip that Zoey would then spread all over town.

"This is Reily Eckardt," Lindy said, gesturing to their companion. "She just moved to town a few months ago. She's engaged to Joe Miller."

If the rock on the cute blonde's finger was any indication, Joe, the owner of Joe's Place, the local bar and grill, was doing quite well for himself.

"Nice to meet you, Caitie," Reily said with a friendly smile. The fact that she already knew Cait's name was a clear sign that she'd been the topic of conversation. She was bound to get that a lot now. That was the way things worked in small towns. If the flow of gossip in Paradise could feed the Foothills Hydro plant in Denver, they would have enough electricity to power the entire state of Colorado for the next fifty years.

"What can I get you ladies?" she asked, then quickly took their orders. Though she promised herself she wouldn't do it, as she walked back to the kitchen, she glanced over at Nate. He sat with near-perfect posture and, because of his broad shoulders, occupied slightly more than his share of space at the counter. He'd been the star running back on the high school football team, and Nate had always been impressively built. But now? She didn't need to see him out of his clothes to know that he was still ripped. His biceps and pecs strained the fabric of his uniform shirt, and his wide shoulders stressed the seams to the limit.

As if he sensed her staring, he turned to look at her. Their eyes met and locked, and his flashed with such naked contempt her stomach did a violent flip-flop.

She forced herself to look away.

Petty as it was, a small part of her had hoped that he would be balding with a spreading waistline. In reality he looked better than he ever had before. At eighteen he had seemed so mature to her, but in reality, he was just a kid. Now, he was *all* man. And then some.

She turned in her order, and when she glanced back

over at Nate a few minutes later, he was gone. She breathed a silent sigh of relief. That could have gone worse, but not much.

He betrayed you, too, she reminded herself, so why did she still feel so darned guilty?

For as long as she could remember, she had been *dependable Caitie,* always doing exactly what was expected of her, sacrificing her own dreams, her own needs, to make everyone else happy. Until one day she had just…snapped. When the acceptance letter to an East Coast school arrived with a full scholarship— one she had only applied for on a whim thinking she would never get it—she knew it was destiny. An opportunity she simply couldn't pass up.

She'd hurt two of the most important people in her life when she'd left so abruptly that fall, and she didn't expect them to understand why she'd done it, but they couldn't hold it against her for the rest of her life. At some point they would have to forgive her.

Right?

Caitie made it through the breakfast rush and was about to sit down for a much-needed break when her dad called her into the back office.

"Would you mind running these papers home to your mom?" he said, handing her a manila folder. "I forgot them last night when I closed up."

She took the folder. "She's not coming in today?"

"She does the bookkeeping and ordering from home now. Her headaches have been much more unpredictable lately, and more frequent."

As long as Caitie could remember her mom had gotten bad headaches. Sometimes two or three a month. "How frequent?"

"A couple times a week."

Caitie sucked in a breath, wondering why she was just now hearing about it. "How long has this been going on?"

"It was a gradual change. I would say that it got really bad this time last year. But now they have her on a new medication. It doesn't take the headache away, but it makes the pain tolerable. And it curbs the nausea."

"There's nothing they can do to stop them?"

He shook his head. "She copes."

Caitie was sure she did. But her mom had worked damned hard all her life. She deserved better than just coping.

Caitie glanced at her watch and said, "I should go, or I'll be late for the lunch rush."

She walked to the row of lockers across from the office to fetch her purse.

"I guess you knew it wasn't going to be easy," he said, leaning in the office doorway, watching her. "Coming back, I mean."

"I guess."

His brow crinkled with concern. "Is there anything I can do?"

"I can handle it," she said, hoping that was true. She slung her purse over her shoulder. "I'll be back before the lunch rush."

"Before you go…" He wrapped her up in a big hug and said, "I love you, Caitie."

It was exactly what she needed. Her dad always knew just what to say and do to make her feel better. "I love you, too, Dad."

She let herself out the back door into the sizzling

August heat, crossed the alley behind the restaurant and climbed into the beat-up Ford compact she'd bought her senior year of high school. The driver's side mirror was secured to the door with duct tape and there was a hole in the dash where the radio used to be, but after all this time it still ran—albeit barely. It took a couple of tries, but the engine sputtered to life and she blasted the air conditioner, which, at its best, spit out air that was more lukewarm than cool. She shut it off and cranked her windows down instead.

She pulled out of the alley and turned left onto Main Street. Her parent's farmhouse, where she was staying, sat on an acre of land a mile north of town. Caitie's great-grandfather, Winston Cavanaugh, who had built the house in the early 1900s, used to own the largest farm in the county and until the Great Depression was one of the wealthiest men in town. But his son—her grandfather George Cavanaugh—having no desire to work the land, sold off all but the one acre her parents now owned and built the diner. Caitie and her younger sister would one day inherit all of it, and would undoubtedly sell it. New York was Cait's home now, and her sister, Kelly, who was attending college in California, was making noises about moving to the West Coast permanently after graduation. Of course, with Kelly, one never knew.

Caitie headed down Main, her car sputtering and coughing it's way past the pharmacy and the thrift store, the post office and the ice-cream shop, marveling at how little things had changed in seven years. She had been home for Christmas and Easter, but she usually avoided venturing into town. Too many memories. Too many questions to answer if she ran into someone she knew.

She passed Joe's Place, a newer, log cabin–style building on the edge of town. The scent of tangy smoking meat was drifting on the air. She flicked her blinker on to swing left onto the county road, but as she made the turn, her car choked and wheezed; then the engine died. She rolled to a stop dead center in the intersection.

She cursed and banged the steering wheel, mumbling, "Please, not today."

She jammed it into Neutral and turned the key, pumping the gas. "Come on, baby, just one more mile."

The engine caught, then roared to life, only to die again before she could get the gear into Drive.

Seriously? As if this day hadn't been miserable enough already.

After several more unsuccessful attempts that only managed to suck whatever juice was left in the battery, she dropped her head against the steering wheel. Sweat beaded her forehead as the temperature in interior of the car skyrocketed.

A car passed, maneuvering around her, and the driver—an older woman Caitie didn't recognize— honked her horn, looking annoyed. Did she honestly think Caitie deliberately stopped in the middle of an intersection? Two more cars went by, their drivers offering her sympathetic smiles, but neither stopped to help. So much for small-town hospitality.

Leaving the car in Neutral, Caitie got out to push it out of the intersection, but pushing and steering simultaneously wasn't as easy as it looked. The soles of her tennis shoes kept slipping on the hot asphalt as she rocked the car, and sweat poured down her face, stinging her eyes. The county road was on a slight decline, so if she could just get the car moving, getting it onto the side of the road should be a piece of cake.

She gave one mighty shove that she knew she would feel later as her back and shoulder muscles screamed in protest. But the car started to roll. Slowly at first, but as she completed the turn onto the county road, it picked up speed as the road dipped down. Her intention was to hop back into the driver's seat and maneuver it onto the side of the road, but she lost her footing. She slipped and went down hard, wincing as her bare knees and palms hit the hot asphalt.

Unfortunately the car kept on going.

She scrambled to her feet, but it was too late. She watched in helpless disbelief as the car accelerated and veered to the right, kicking up dust as it hit the shoulder. Then it plunged into the ditch dividing the road from Mr. Johnson's cornfield and with a sickening crunch of metal landed ass end up.

The situation was so ridiculous, she didn't know if she should laugh or cry or pinch herself to wake up from this horrible nightmare.

She walked toward the wreck, her knees stinging, her back aching. Yet she felt oddly detached, as if she were watching the situation unfold from outside her own body.

She was a few yards from the car when she heard another vehicle coming down the road behind her. Maybe this time someone would stop to help her.

The patrol car passed her, slowing as it reached her car. The driver made a sharp U-turn, swung onto the opposite shoulder and parked.

With the sun reflecting off the windshield she couldn't make out the occupant. *Please God, let it be anyone but him.*

The door swung open, and she watched in dismay as Nate unfolded his large frame from the car.

She mumbled a curse and thought, *This really is not my day.*

Chapter Two

When he'd left the diner that morning, Nate had vowed to avoid Caitie whenever humanly possible. But when the call came in about the car stalled in the intersection, he'd had no idea it would be her.

He would have driven past and kept going, but this was a matter of public safety, and as an officer of the law he had an obligation to stop and assist her. Though how she had managed to get her car from the intersection to the ditch was a mystery.

He radioed for a tow, then got out and crossed the road to Caitie's car. It sat nose down in a tangle of weeds and grass in the ditch. Caitie, looking alarmingly disheveled with her sweat-soaked hair and clothes and bleeding knees, limped over and joined him.

Suddenly his bad day didn't seem so horrible after all.

Shoulders slumped, looking tired and defeated, Caitie stopped beside him, gazing down into the ditch at what was left of her car. From what he could see, the front end was in pretty bad shape but probably fixable. Although, considering the age of the car, it hardly seemed worth it. Honestly, it was a miracle it still ran at all.

"You look like hell," he told her.

Without taking her eyes off the car, she said, "Thanks for noticing."

"Are you okay?"

"Define 'okay.'"

"Are you in need of medical assistance?"

She shook her head. "I'll live."

"So, you want to tell me what happened?"

She shook her head again and said, "No. Not really."

"I need to fill out an accident report."

Her attention shot to him. "It wasn't an accident."

"You put your car in a ditch on purpose?"

She rolled her eyes in exasperation. "Of course not! It died, and I was…pushing it out of the road."

The mental picture almost made him smile. "Got away from you, did it?"

Her deadpan look was the only answer he required.

As much as he wanted to believe she deserved it, wanted to feel vindicated, she looked so damned defeated he couldn't manage anything but pity. He'd been so busy not looking at her in the diner, he hadn't noticed the dark circles under her eyes, or that she was thinner than he'd even seen her. Her wrists looked bony and her collarbones jutted out.

But whatever she'd suffered, or was still suffering,

she'd brought it on herself. That was what he wanted to believe, anyway.

Caitie stepped forward to climb down the embankment, and without thinking he grabbed her upper arm to stop her. The instant his fingers touched her bare skin, he was hit by a zap of awareness so intense it nearly knocked him into the road.

Where in the hell had *that* come from?

Considering the way Caitie blinked in surprise and jerked her arm free, she must have felt it, too. "At ease, Officer."

"You can't go down there," he said.

"I have to get my things."

"It may not be safe. You should wait until the tow truck gets here."

"I haven't called one."

"I did. It shouldn't be more than an hour."

"I don't have an hour. I have to get back to work. And there are papers in there from the diner that my mom needs now. And I need my purse."

"Where is it?"

"Everything was on the front passenger seat."

With a sigh of resignation he told her, "Stay here."

Hands propped on her hips, she scowled. "I didn't ask for your help."

Like it or not, she was getting it. If she went down there and wound up hurting herself, it would be his ass on the line. He picked his way down the slope into the ditch on the passenger's side of the car, weeds twisting around his legs and clinging to his uniform pants like tentacles. Thankfully there had been no rain for a while, or he would be trudging through mud and muck.

He gave the car a firm shove, to make sure it was

stable, and it didn't budge. From this angle he could see that the hood was wedged under a large boulder at the edge of the field. This car had definitely seen its last days on the road.

"How bad is it?" she called down to him.

"Looks fatal," he answered, and he heard her mutter something under her breath. "Sorry, I missed that."

"I said, *what next?* Which in retrospect was probably a stupid idea. Why tempt fate?"

He didn't believe in fate. Not anymore.

He tried the passenger's side door. It resisted at first, but with one hard yank and the grating screech of metal against metal, it opened. As he leaned inside he was filled with an eerie sense of déjà vu. Somehow, despite having essentially spent the past seven years under a tarp in the garage, the car still smelled like the coconut body spray she'd used in high school.

He shook the thought away as he reached over and switched on the hazard lights.

The papers she'd mentioned lay scattered across the floor. He gathered them up, revealing an expensive-looking leather purse underneath, its contents spilled out onto the mat. He recognized the brand as one his ex-wife had often coveted but could never afford.

He had overheard his dad tell someone that Caitie had done rather well for herself in New York. It was a surprise to Nate. Not because he considered her incompetent. He had just always believed that material things didn't interest her, that family was what she really cared about. Living in the city had obviously changed her.

Or hell, maybe he never really knew her at all.

He slid the sheets of paper—which looked to be financial forms—back into their folder and stuffed her belongings back into her purse. He gave the interior a final cursory glance, a disturbing sense of longing tugging at his soul. He shut the door and climbed out of the ditch.

"Thank you," she said when he reached the top and handed her things over. "I could have gotten them."

He should have let her do just that, but he had been entrusted by the town to keep its residents safe, and it was a duty he took very seriously. So, until Caitie went back to New York, she was essentially his to protect.

"I noticed your left taillight is still flickering," he told her, looking back at the car.

"Only because *someone* never got around to fixing it for me," she said sharply. "Though he promised about a hundred times."

Resentment churned his gut. Who was this woman? The Caitie he knew had always been so sweet and accommodating, so…nice. She never had a negative thing to say about anyone. Well, almost never.

"I'm not the only one who made promises," he reminded her. She had promised to marry him and have his children and spend the rest of her life with him.

Yet here they were, *not married*.

"Can I go now?" she asked.

He wasn't sure where his reply originated, maybe from some deep dark place where the pain still simmered, but it was out of his mouth before he could stop it. "Leaving *is* what you do best."

Her sharp intake of breath said the barb had struck its target. He waited for the feeling of satisfaction to release the weight that had been dragging him down since he'd first heard her voice in the diner. But treating women with respect was a virtue so deeply engrained by his parents, he felt like a jerk instead.

Her bluster and bravado seemed to leak away, filing the edge off her sharp tongue. "I didn't want to hurt you, Nate. If you believe anything, please believe that."

Whether she meant to or not, she *had* hurt him. She'd left with no regard for anyone else's feelings. Abandoned him and all their friends with no logical explanation.

If this was her lame attempt at an apology, she was wasting her time. It was too late for that. She'd betrayed his trust, and, whatever her excuse, that would never be okay with him.

"Let's go sit in my car," he said.

Looking apprehensive, she asked, "What for?"

"It beats standing in the hot sun while I write this up."

She hugged the file to her chest, shooting an anxious glance down the county road, as if she were plotting an escape route. Did she think she could outrun him? "I told you what happened. Do I really need to be here?"

Was she in such a rush to get back to the diner, or just eager to get away from him? It didn't matter either way. His priority was to do his job.

"I'll need your statement. Then you'll have to sign it, so yes," he told her. "You do, in fact, need to be here."

Caitie realized that she was in no position to be asking Nate for any favors, but it couldn't hurt to try.

Swallowing the crumbs of her shredded pride, she said, "Could we maybe skip the report this time? I mean, no one was hurt, right? No one else was even *involved*. So who would know?"

He just stared at her with his "cop" expression.

"If I'm late back to the restaurant, it's everyone else who will suffer. The waitresses, the customers. My dad."

"Maybe you should have considered that when you drove your car into the ditch."

Like she had done it on purpose. And technically, she'd *pushed* it in. If the damned car hadn't stalled, she wouldn't be in this mess.

Nate crossed the road to his cruiser and opened the back door. It was silly to believe that he would cut her any slack after all that had happened.

She waited for a truck to rumble past, then walked across the road and peered into the cruiser. "I have to sit in back, locked in like a criminal?"

"Those are the rules," he said.

It wasn't as if she'd never been in the back of a police vehicle. Nate's dad, P.J., a state police officer, had sometimes given them rides in his squad car. But this was different. Once she got in there, she would be trapped. Not that she thought he would hurt her. Not physically anyway. But he could spoon-feed her all the bitterness and resentment that had obviously built up these past years, and she would have no choice but to swallow it.

She stepped closer, then hesitated. Did she really want to do this?

Did she have a choice?

The longer she stalled, the later she'd be getting back to work. And there was nothing she hated more than letting people down. Though it was getting to be a recurring theme for her. First she let everyone down by leaving Paradise, then she let down her clients by not seeing the fraud going on right under her nose.

She glanced up at Nate as she slipped into the car, and as their eyes met, his were so cold and emotionless, it was as if he were looking right through her. She'd seen that look before.

Nate rarely lost his temper or even raised his voice—or he didn't when they were younger. His weapon was silence. And the less he talked, the more she felt the need to justify herself over whatever it was he was upset about, which would usually leave her feeling like the bad guy. Whether it was her fault or not.

Not anymore.

He shut the door and walked around the vehicle. With every step he took, her anxiety mounted. She glanced at her watch. There was no way she would make it back in time for the lunch rush now. Thanks to her carelessness, and foot dragging, everyone else at the diner would have to pick up the slack.

Nate climbed into the car, his eyes cold and hard as he glanced at her in the rearview mirror. Well, she wasn't so thrilled seeing him again, either. If she had her choice, she would still be in New York, but the money in her savings account could be stretched a whole lot further staying in Paradise rent-free.

She would never forget opening her office door to find the halls swarming with agents from the Federal Trade Commission, and watching in shock as the CEO was led out in handcuffs. Immediately rumors began to fly that the firm had direct ties to the mob and had been defrauding some of its wealthiest clients for years. A virtual pyramid scam.

Suddenly she and her coworkers found themselves thrust into the center of a federal investigation. The CFO had gone missing that day, along with millions of dollars, and still hadn't been located. Caitie figured that there were two likely scenarios. Either he was on a beach in Aruba sipping mai tais, or had been laid to rest somewhere in Jersey under a concrete slab.

Her money was on Jersey.

Nate was silent for so long, and so still, she wondered if she should check for a pulse. When he did finally speak, the sound of his voice startled her.

"If I let you go now, do you promise to come by the station in the morning and file a report?"

He was cutting her a break? Seriously? She sat up a little straighter as her heart lifted. "Yes! Absolutely I'll do that. I promise."

His eyes narrowed. "Eight a.m.? Before I go out on patrol."

"I'll be there. You have my word."

She braced herself for a crack about her word not meaning much to him, but it never came.

"For the record, I'm doing this for Lou," he told her. "Not you. So don't forget."

"I won't."

He did a U-turn onto the road and headed in the direction of her parents' house. She was getting a free pass *and* a ride home? This was unprecedented.

She studied his profile as he drove silently down the county road. Eyes forward, lips sealed in a rigid line. From this angle he looked exactly as he had in high school, and she felt a pang somewhere deep in her chest. A sudden longing for the way things used to be. But they were not, nor would they ever be, a couple. She had her life in New York, and he had his in Paradise. *And never the twain shall meet.*

Not often anyway. In fact, she hoped that tomorrow at the station would be the last she saw of him. She anticipated that the headhunter would call soon with good news and she could go back to New York.

Nate didn't say a word as he pulled up her parents' long gravel driveway and rolled to a stop close to the side door. The three-car detached garage was open and her mom's car was parked inside. Maybe Caitie could con a ride back to the diner from her.

This being the first time she had seen the house in true daylight since she'd arrived, she took a good look around. Was it her imagination or were things looking a little…run-down?

Despite the hours they worked, her parents had always seen that the house and yard were meticulously cared for. Even if that meant hiring one of the local kids to mow the grass. Caitie had been too busy with work and school to do it, and if Kelly had been handcuffed to the mower she would find an excuse to get out of it.

The once white siding on the house had weathered to a dull gray, and the trim around the windows was peeling in places. The front flower beds were dry and scrubby and overgrown, more weeds than flowers. The vegetable garden was in no better shape. She saw only a few straggly plants that looked as if they had come up on their own from seed.

As long as Caitie had been alive, they planted the garden every spring, and in the fall her mom would take a couple of days off work to can the crop. She would put up pickles, relish and dilly beans and several varieties of hot peppers. In the fall they went apple picking at a local orchard so her mom could make sauce. The all-natural chunky kind with no added sugar. Until she was away at school Caitie had never even tried store-bought applesauce. There was no comparison.

She wondered if she could help her parents out by tidying up the yard, planting a flat or two of flowers. Marigolds had always been her mom's favorite. The front porch could stand a good scrubbing and a fresh coat of paint, as well. As could the siding and the trim. Heck, she might as well paint it all, and totally re-landscape the yard. It would be the perfect project to keep her occupied while she was there. Something constructive to do. She'd always hoped that someday she would have time to explore her creative side. Maybe this was her chance.

She waited for Nate to get out and open her door, but he just sat there, eyes forward, not moving or making a sound. Had he forgotten that she was locked in?

She cleared her throat, hoping to catch his attention, but he didn't budge. It was as if he'd forgotten she was back there.

After another minute or so, her patience began to wear thin. He knew she was in a hurry. Why would he let her postpone the police report, drive her home, then keep her trapped in his backseat?

If he needed to say something, she wished he would just spit it out.

"Penny for your thoughts," she said, taking a stab at a little lighthearted humor.

He cut his eyes to her in the mirror, looking anything but amused.

"Or not," she mumbled.

His expression was so empty, so lacking in emotion, he could have been cast from wax had his mouth not been moving. "I used to think if I ever saw you again, the only thing I would want to know is *why*. But now that you're here, now that we've come face-to-face, I realize…" He looked back at her over his shoulder. "I don't care anymore."

Ouch. Whether or not hurting her had been his goal, that remark cut deep. Not that she had expected him to be miserable, alone and still pining for her, unable to move on with his life. But a girl could hope, right?

She banished that thought to somewhere deep down where it belonged. And having said his piece—short though effective as it had been—Nate finally got out and opened her door.

As she was climbing out, her battered knees protesting with a deep, stinging ache, she heard the side door on the house creak open. She looked over to see her mom standing on the back porch.

In Cait's opinion, her mom, Betty, was as pretty now as she had been at seventeen, when she won the Miss Denver beauty pageant. She was thirty years older now, and a little bit softer around the edges, but she still had that spark. It had been difficult as a child, growing up in a household with females as beautiful as her mom and sister. No one ever came right out and told Caitie she was aesthetically inferior, but she knew.

Caitie sometimes wondered if her mom ever regretted not doing more with her life. During her stint as a beauty queen, a Chicago-based modeling agency had offered her a two-year contract. She could have had an exciting career in the city, but instead she chose to stay in Paradise, get married and work at the diner.

Gauging by her stunned expression, seeing Caitie with Nate was probably the last thing her mom expected on Caitie's first day back.

"Hello, Nate," she said, looking quizzically from him to Caitie. But as Caitie stepped out from behind the car door and her mom saw her disheveled appearance, including the dried blood caked on her knees, she gasped and clasped a hand to her bosom. "What on earth happened to you?"

Caitie had never been one to resort to sarcasm to make a point, but what the heck. "Nate and I were just getting reacquainted," she said, smiling when she heard him grumble under his breath.

He never used to grumble.

"I'm going to assume that was a joke," her mom said, though she looked as if she wasn't sure.

"See ya, Betty," Nate said, then narrowed his cop stare on Caitie. "Eight a.m. *Don't* forget."

Like she could forget that. "Thanks for the ride, Deputy Jefferies."

He shot her a look.

Had he or had he not insisted that she address him by his rank? Now he didn't like it?

Nate grumbled something incoherent as he got in the cruiser and drove away. He never used to grumble, and he sure did seem to frown a lot now. Perhaps the serious nature of his profession had jaded him.

But this was Paradise, where there was barely any crime to be jaded about.

Caitie turned back to her mom, who stood patiently awaiting an explanation.

"So," she asked, looking Caitie up and down. "Rough morning?"

Feeling exhausted, as if she'd just worked a week of double shifts, when in reality it was barely eleven, Caitie sighed and said, "You have no idea."

Chapter Three

"Let's get you cleaned up," her mom said, and Caitie followed her into the house. A pot simmered on the stove, and the scent of spicy tomato sauce hung heavy in the air.

At least the inside of her parents' house hadn't changed much. The furniture was older, the carpet worn in places, but the house was neat as a pin.

"Maybe you could tell me what really happened," her mom suggested, lifting the lid and giving the sauce a quick stir. "Like how you hurt your knees."

Caitie slumped into a kitchen chair. "You think this is bad, you should see the other guy."

Her mom blinked. "Other guy?"

"I'm kidding. I did this to myself. Literally."

"Where is your car? And why did Nate drive you home?"

"My car is dead in the ditch off the county road just past town. By the Johnsons' field."

"I see." Her mom grabbed the first-aid kit from the top shelf of the pantry and set it on the counter, pulling out everything she needed. "*How* did it get into the ditch?"

"I pushed it there." Her mom's brows lifted in surprise, and Caitie quickly added, "And, no, I did *not* do it on purpose. It died in the middle of the intersection. I was trying to move it out of the way."

Caitie gave her mom the short version of what had happened while she cleaned her knees. She was kind enough not to laugh, but she did crack a smile when Caitie described watching helplessly as the car plunged into the ditch.

"Why did you leave the diner?" her mom asked.

"To give you the—" Caitie closed her eyes and groaned. She'd left the damned folder in the backseat of Nate's cruiser.

Really? All that for *nothing*.

"The what?" her mom asked, soaking a cotton ball with antiseptic.

"The papers dad sent home."

She looked confused. "Papers?"

Caitie sucked in a breath as her mom dabbed her knees and the antiseptic burned her raw skin. "From the restaurant. Didn't he call you?"

She was quiet for a second, as if she was trying to recall. "Oh, right. *Those* papers. He must have forgotten to call."

"Well, I left them in Nathan's car by accident."

"Oh, don't worry about it. It's nothing urgent." She swabbed antibiotic ointment on the scratches, then smoothed a large bandage over each knee. "There you go. Good as new. More or less."

"Thanks, Mom."

"Be sure to take the bandages off when the bleeding stops. The more air the scrapes get, the faster they'll heal."

"I'll take them off tonight before bed." She stood, wincing when she caught a glimpse of her reflection in the glass on the side door. "I'm a mess. I need to put a clean uniform on before I go back to the diner. I'm sure glad those things still fit me." They were even a bit loose on her. Thanks to the stress of being unemployed, she hadn't had much of an appetite lately.

"You don't have to go back," her mom said. "Deb is feeling better so she'll finish out her shift."

Confused, Caitie asked her, "How do you know that?"

"Your father told me, of course."

"Dad called?"

"Yes, after you left the restaurant."

Huh? "Mom, a minute ago you said that he *didn't* call."

She blinked. "No, I didn't."

"Yes, you did. You said that he must have forgotten to call."

Her mom sighed and shook her head. "I'm sorry. It's this darned migraine medicine. It makes me loopy sometimes. What I meant was, he forgot to *tell* me about the papers. But, yes, he did call."

That must have been some powerful stuff she was taking. "So, I'm off the hook?"

"Yes, he's all set for the day shift."

As much as she wanted to help her parents, she

was relieved. It was too much too soon. "I do have a few errands to run. Although I no longer have a car to run them with."

Her mom tucked the first-aid kit back into the pantry. "Take my car—I won't be using it."

"Are you sure?"

"But only if you promise to bring home a gallon of milk. We ran out last night."

At first she thought her mom was kidding, since she had been the one to send Caitie out that morning. "Mom, you know I got the milk already."

"You did?"

This was no joke. Her blank expression said she had no idea what Caitie was talking about. "Remember, I forgot the diner key, and it was so early everything in town was still closed, so I had to drive all the way to the twenty-four-hour store at the service station on the highway."

With a frown her mom pulled the fridge open, and there on the shelf sat the gallon of 2 percent milk. "Darned medication," she muttered. "I would lose a limb if they weren't all sewn on."

"Do they have any idea what's causing you to have so many headaches?"

"It could be a hormone imbalance, since it seems to coincide with menopause."

"Have you thought to try homeopathic remedies? Holistic medicine? Maybe you could try cutting processed foods from your diet. Or gluten."

"I'll definitely consider that," she said, though to Caitie it sounded as if her mom was humoring her.

Her mom walked to the stove and lifted the lid off the pan, giving the sauce another stir. She looked fine, but something just seemed…off. Something other than chronic headaches.

"Is everything okay?" Caitie asked.

Her mom turned to her and smiled. "Of course, honey."

She sounded genuine, so why didn't Caitie believe her? Could she and Caitie's dad be having problems?

Her parents had always had a good marriage. Sure, they argued occasionally. What couple didn't? Mostly about money or the diner. But Caitie's mom had always seemed happy with her modest, small-town life. At least, that was the way it had always appeared to Caitie.

When Caitie had presented her mom with her college acceptance letter, and finally had the courage to admit her plan to move to the East Coast, her mom's reaction had surprised her.

"If you want out of this town, if you want something more from life, leave while you can," her mom had told her. "Don't let anything or anyone hold you back."

Caitie had done exactly that, but her mom's words haunted her for months afterward. Had it been her way of saying she regretted giving up the chance at a lucrative and prestigious modeling career to stay in Paradise? And had that regret begun to cause a rift in her parents' relationship?

She would ask her sister what she knew, but Kelly had been so self-absorbed with school and her very active social life, she wouldn't see a tsunami coming until it crashed down over her head. No that was unfair. Kelly had *always* been self-absorbed. She had inherited their mother's beauty and her pinup model figure. She had always been the pretty one. Not that

Caitie had gone three rounds with an ugly stick. She was attractive in an average way. Pleasant to look at, but nothing to get all excited about.

There had been times when she wondered what it was that Nate saw in her, when there were other girls—prettier girls—who would have given anything to be with him. Those first few months of dating him, she'd lived in a constant state of flux. Happy beyond her wildest dreams, yet always waiting for the ax to fall. For him to realize how much better he could do. She truly believed it was only a matter of time before he dumped her and moved on to someone else.

Her mom replaced the pan lid and set down the spoon, saying offhandedly, "So, did anything interesting happen at the diner this morning?"

Way to be subtle, Mom. "Did Dad tell you?"

"We talked," she admitted. "He said there was tension."

A minimalist point of view. "Dad was being kind."

Her mom winced. "It was that bad?"

"At first Nate wouldn't even *look* at me. Like he thought he would turn into a pillar of salt should our eyes meet."

"What did you expect?" she asked, looking puzzled. "A hug?"

Caitie blinked. Whose side was she on? "No, of course not. But—"

"You knew you would see him. You had time to prepare. Imagine if Nate had just suddenly shown up unannounced. Would you have reacted any differently?"

She sighed. "Probably not."

"It's also possible that deep down he still has feelings for you."

"He has feelings all right. He *hates* me."

"He did stop to help you."

"Only because he *had* to. It's his job. It was obvious he didn't want to be there."

"He drove you home. And let you wait to fill out a report. He didn't have to do that."

Let's give him a medal. "Why does it seem as if everyone is on *his* side? Yes, I left, and I didn't do it very well, but I spent most of those first few months miserable, lonely and missing him, while *he* was back home knocking up and marrying my best friend."

"Just remember that there are two sides to every story."

"I don't care about his story. It's done. I'm over it. I've moved on."

"It seems to me that if you had truly moved on, you wouldn't care what Nate did or didn't do."

Oh, ouch. A direct hit. And the worst part? She was right. When it came to speaking her mind, Betty Cavanaugh rarely held back. She didn't sugarcoat either, sometimes making her keen observations a bitter pill to swallow.

"I really hate it when you use your Vulcan logic on me," Caitie said, dropping her chin in her hand. She wouldn't bother trying to deny that she and Nate had unresolved issues. Issues that *he* clearly had *no* desire to work through. And she just flat out didn't see the point. They'd had their inevitable, awkward confrontation—which, if anything, made matters worse—and now it was over. The trick was to avoid him as long as she was here, and then, after she'd returned to New York and got back to her *real* life, she could forget all about him.

As if.

After seven years, she still hadn't figured out how.

"Any plans for the rest of the day?" her mom asked, and Caitie was grateful for the change of subject.

"Job hunting." Caitie grabbed an energy drink from the fridge, but as she was walking through the doorway to the living room, she had a thought. She stopped and turned back to the stove, where her mom was stirring the sauce again. "Just out of curiosity, Mom. Why did Dad send those papers home to you?"

Her mom blinked, looking confused. "What do you mean?"

"Couldn't he have just brought them home tonight? Since you said yourself it was nothing urgent. Or better yet, why didn't he just email then to the home computer?"

Her mom sighed, realizing the jig was up. "Your dad said you were very upset after seeing Nate. He just wanted an excuse to get you out of the diner. But he knew if he tried to give you the rest of the day off you would balk."

He was right. "Did Deb really come back early, or did he have to find someone else to cover the rest of the shift?"

"He called someone in. Though I'm sure he wouldn't have sent you home if he knew it would become such a fiasco."

"I could have worked. Yes, I was upset, but I would have gotten over it."

"He was just trying to help."

She knew that, and she loved him for it. But she was a grown woman now, and this was one problem she needed to figure out on her own.

* * *

On his way back to the station, Nate checked his phone, which had been ringing almost nonstop for the past thirty minutes or so, and saw that his ex-wife, Melanie, had left him three messages. He didn't have to hear them to know what they were concerning. Paradise was a hotbed of gossip, and Mel's salon was the main hub, with Simmons Hardware trailing at a close second.

Nate stuffed his phone back in his pocket. This was a conversation they needed to have face-to-face.

He drove to the salon and steered his cruiser into an open spot on the street out front. The door jingled and the stench of acetone and perm solution assaulted him as he stepped inside. Being the only salon within ten miles, business was steady. All but one of the six hair stations had customers and two nail techs worked on manicures. Meaning fourteen pairs of curious eyes settled on him.

Clearly everyone had heard the news.

Nate usually took comfort in the fact that when he walked down the street, or entered a local business, nearly every face there was a familiar one. Today, he longed for a modicum of anonymity. Or at the very least, a little personal space.

"Good morning, ladies," he said.

Mel stood at her station finishing a comb-out on Mrs. Samuels, who at ninety-two still kept her flat black hair teased into a beehive and sprayed to the consistency of fiberglass. Which not only added six inches to her four-foot-eleven-inch frame, but gave her papery skin an ethereal, grayish cast. Nate had seen corpses with more color. Once, a few years back, when Mrs. Samuels had dozed off under the dryer, she was so pale that Mel thought she had shuffled loose the mortal coil right there in the salon. Everyone had been too weirded out to try and wake her. Ultimately they'd held a hand mirror under her nose to make sure she was still breathing.

Regina, one of the stylists, smiled sympathetically at Nate and said, "We all heard."

One sharp look from Mel shut her down, but Nate could feel the silent tension growing.

"All finished, Miz Samuels," Mel said loudly, helping her client up from the chair. Mrs. Samuels was by no means spry, but considering her advanced age she still got around fairly well. At least once a day she could be seen tooling around town in her mint condition, canary-yellow 1970 Mustang Fastback. A gift from her husband, Walter—God rest his saintly soul— on her forty-fifth birthday.

As Mel opened the door for her, her eyes snagged on Nathan's and a silent understanding passed between them. He followed her through the salon, past the nail techs and washbowls to her office in the back.

When they were inside, she closed and locked the door, then leaned against it. "Are you okay? As soon as I heard I called to warn you, but you didn't answer. You saw her at the diner?"

"Yes. And I'm fine," he told her.

She lifted a questioning brow.

He sighed. If there was one person he trusted with his true feelings, it was Mel. They were best friends. "Okay, I'm *coping.*"

"I guess we both knew Caitie coming back was a possibility."

Yet they had never discussed how they would handle it if she did. An oversight he now regretted.

"How does she look?" Mel asked. She had once admitted to Nate that deep down she had always been a little jealous of Caitie. It had seemed to Mel that all the good stuff happened to her best friend. She did better in school than Mel, who, like their son, had a mild form of dyslexia. Caitie's hair, a natural pale honey blond, always seemed to fall perfectly into place with hardly any effort while Mel had to wrestle with her naturally curly auburn locks for an hour every morning. Caitie's creamy smooth complexion had been flawless while Mel battled teenage acne and oily skin. Caitie was also tall, slender and lithe, and never had to watch what she ate. Mel was forever battling the bulge and swore she gained weight just looking at food. And no matter how many times he told her she was beautiful—which she was, both inside and out—she'd wrestled with her insecurities. And still did, which is why he chose his next words very carefully.

"She looks…the same." He didn't mention her weight, since it was such a sore spot with Mel. She had tried every diet craze and exercise gimmick known to man, yet she never lost more than ten or fifteen pounds. Which was twenty to twenty-five pounds less than she wanted to lose.

A deck chair off the Titanic, she'd called it.

"I heard she's in some sort of trouble," Mel said. "Someone even suggested that she's on the run from the FBI."

He'd heard that, too, when he stopped by the station after breakfast. But no one as intelligent as Caitie would be dense enough to hide from law enforcement in her hometown right under her parents' roof. And if there were a manhunt to find her, as local law enforcement, he would have heard about it by now. "I seriously doubt that."

"So she's probably not going into witness protection, either," Mel said.

"Not that I'm aware."

"Do you know how long she's staying?"

Hopefully not long. "Nope."

Mel gnawed her bottom lip. "What was it like to see her again?"

He shrugged and told a little white lie. "It was disturbing to see her again...at first. But now I don't feel much of anything about it."

"This could get awkward," she said. "And *complicated.*"

Story of his life.

"I'm not going to let it come between us," he assured her. "Our friendship means more to me than Caitie ever could."

She didn't look as if she believed him. "I was invisible to you until she left."

"Mel—"

She stopped him midsentence, brushing away the tear that leaked down her cheek. "That wasn't fair, I know. Please, ignore me. I'm feeling sorry for myself. I just can't help thinking, now that she's back, you're going to forget all about me and Cody."

"That will *never* happen." He pulled Mel into his arms and kissed the top of her head, his heart hurting for her, wishing he could have loved her as something other than a friend. He did try, but after six months of marriage counseling, even the therapist agreed they would be better off as partners in parenting and good friends. Divorce had been the only viable option if they had any hope of preserving their friendship. It hadn't been easy, but they were in a good place now. And to this day he had no regrets, not when he looked at their son. "If Caitie never left, Cody wouldn't even exist."

"That's true," she said.

Nate never knew how much he wanted to be a father until he watched his son being born, held him for the very first time. He had been totally unplanned, and three weeks premature. And so tiny and fragile Nate had been terrified he might drop him. Cody had gazed up at Nate with the wisdom and patience of a very old soul, as if to say, *Don't worry, you'll do just fine. I have faith in you.*

Nate fell instantly in love and from that day forward, his boy was all that mattered. Nate knew the first time he held his son that he was destined for great things. And now, at six years old, Cody had an innate patience and a deep understanding of people that left adults scratching their heads. Sometimes he would get this look, as if he knew something no one else did. And though his reading difficulties set him apart from other kids his age, he took it all in stride.

"Are you still in love with her?" Mel asked, her voice muffled against Nate's shirt.

The question was so out of the blue, so ridiculous, he snapped his head back hard enough to give himself whiplash. "I can't believe you asked me that."

She looked up at him, her eyes—which could never decide if they wanted to be blue or green—swimming with tears. "Is it really that unusual a question? You loved her before."

"Without trust, there can be no love."

"You never got closure. Neither of us have." Her arms tightened around him. "Now I'm so confused. This morning, when Regina told me Caitie was back, my first instinct was to run down to the diner, throw my arms around her and hug her. I was actually excited at the idea of seeing her, and for a split second I desperately wanted my best friend back."

Mel's first instinct involved hugs and reconciliation. The only thing Nate had wanted to do was hurl. That had to mean something, didn't it? "If that's how you feel, maybe you should talk to her."

"I'm not sure what I feel. I never imagined that her coming back could be so—"

"Disruptive," he finished for her.

"Yes! It's all I can think about. I'm so preoccupied I nearly used the wrong color dye on Mrs. Newburg."

"For what it's worth, seeing her for the short amount of time that I did made me realize that we're two completely different people now. She's changed." It had seemed that way to him at least. Or maybe that was what he preferred to believe. He resented her coming back and disrupting the quiet, orderly life that he had spent the past seven years building. She had no right.

"No matter what happens with Caitie, you and Cody will always be the most important people in the world to me."

"I know."

He held his ex-wife close, wishing there was something he could say, a way he could assure her everything would be okay and nothing would change.

Only problem was, things had begun to change already.

Chapter Four

"Let her die with dignity," Jake—of Jake's Garage—told Caitie later that evening after supper.

"The front end is pretty smashed up," she said, surprised that so much damage had been done at such a low speed.

"That's not even the worst of it." He lifted the hood. "Your block is cracked."

She didn't really know what that meant, but it didn't sound good. "So what you're saying is, it's definitely not worth fixing."

"I wouldn't waste my money."

She trusted his judgment. It wasn't the first time her car had been to that garage. Jake had worked on it years ago when his dad owned the business. Jake Senior retired and of course Jake Junior took over. That was the way it worked in Paradise. When the parent retired, the oldest child took over. And in Jake's case, they didn't even have to change the sign.

"What should I do with it now?" she asked him.

He slammed the hood and wiped his hands on the greasy rag hanging from the pocket of his pants. "I know a guy who owns a junkyard. He'd take it off your hands, give you a hundred bucks cash for it."

Someone would actually pay her cash for this pile of junk? "That would be awesome. What do I owe you for looking at it?"

"It was fifty bucks for the tow. No charge to look at it."

So she would actually make money on the deal? *Go figure.* Granted not *much* money, but these days every penny counted.

"Do you take Visa?" she asked Jake.

"Sure do. Let's go in the office."

Back in high school Caitie's car hadn't been the most reliable thing on four wheels, so she had seen the inside of the garage office enough times to know that virtually nothing had changed. He had the same grimy cash register that had gone out of date sometime in the past century, printed ads on the walls for car products that dated back to before she was born, and the entire office was covered in a fine coat of greasy dust. Even the floor felt sticky under her flip-flops. And though she wasn't sure what color the walls were originally, now they were a filthy grayish-yellow.

She watched Jake fill out the paperwork. His hands were dry and calloused with painful-looking cracks on his knuckles and grease caked under his nails.

"Fifty bucks even," he said, and she handed him her credit card.

"When did your dad retire?" she asked as he ran the charge.

"Three years ago." He gave her the slip to sign, then handed over her receipt, leaving a greasy fingerprint on the edge. "You'll need to sign the title over."

"I'll have to find it." She was sure her mom had it filed away somewhere safe. "So, do you like owning the business?"

Leaning with one hip propped against the counter, he shrugged. "It is what it is. What else am I gonna do?"

She wanted to say, *Hey, I got out, and you can, too.* But she would probably just insult him, or come off as uppity. Besides, she wasn't exactly the poster child for making it in the big city. What Jake did with his life—or didn't do—was none of her business.

They chatted for a few more minutes, mostly about superficial things. He'd been four years ahead of her in school, so they didn't have many friends in common. She was a little relieved when she finally said goodbye and left the garage.

Many of the businesses in town closed their doors at five, but the thrift store stayed open until nine on weekdays. Needing several personal items to get her through the next few weeks, Cait parked her mom's car in the street and walked the two blocks. She encountered a few familiar faces, but with a baseball cap hiding her hair and dark sunglasses shading her eyes, no one seemed to recognize her.

As she stepped through the automatic door, a wall of cool air enveloped her. The thrift store, as with the rest of town, hadn't changed much, and it was practically deserted.

She took a quick look around to get her bearings, then located the personal care aisle exactly where it had been the last time she'd visited.

She walked briskly to the aisle and grabbed a cheap bottle of both shampoo and conditioner and a package of disposable razors. Next she headed to the toy/gardening aisle, hoping to find some sort of book on landscaping.

About halfway down the aisle, an adorable, tow-headed little boy with curly hair stood intently studying a display of Legos, most of which were on a high shelf just out of his reach.

"Do you need help reaching something?" Caitie asked, and he turned to look at her with bright green inquisitive eyes. Eyes that narrowed suspiciously as he gave her the once-over. She put him at seven or eight years old, and something about him seemed distinctly familiar, though she was almost positive she had never met him.

"I'm not a'sposed to talk to strangers," he said, so matter-of-factly it made her smile. Smart kid.

"I'm Caitie," she said, taking off her sunglasses, thinking it would make her look less intimidating.

Like a lightbulb switching on, recognition lit his face. "You're the lady in the pictures," he said.

"Pictures?" Feeling suddenly self-conscious, she shoved her sunglasses back on. "What pictures?"

"In the box in Daddy's closet."

Uh-oh. There was only one man in town who would have any reason to have photos of her in his closet. She suddenly realized why the boy looked so familiar.

"Shopping incognito?" a familiar voice said from behind her.

She winced and the spaghetti she'd eaten for dinner tossed around in her stomach. *Three* times in one day? What were the odds? Paradise was a small town, but come on.

She turned to Nate, who was in his street clothes—a pair of navy chino shorts and a white polo shirt. In one hand he held a package of cookies, and in the other a box of tampons, of all things.

"Great disguise," he said.

Not so great that he hadn't recognized her. "Now I get it," she said.

"Get what?"

"Why you were so cranky this morning." She gestured to the items he was holding. "PMS."

"Daddy, what's PMS?" Cody asked.

He shot Caitie a look, then cut his eyes back to his son. "Never mind, Cody."

Cody was a miniature version of Nate but with Mel's striking green eyes. Caitie couldn't help wondering, if she and Nate had stayed together and had a child, who would it look like? Him? Her? A combination of the two?

What was the point in wondering about something that never had and never would happen? Only a man smitten with a woman would buy her feminine products, meaning he must be involved with someone new.

She wrote off the sudden churning in her belly as indigestion, when the truth was, it felt a lot more like jealousy. And that was unacceptable. But rather than walk away, she heard herself ask, "So, I hear you keep pictures of me in a box in your closet."

Only after the words were out did she realize that she may have just ratted Cody out. What if he wasn't supposed to be snooping in his dad's closet? But if Nate was angry he didn't let it show, nor did he justify her accusation with a response. Cody didn't even seem to notice. He was back to staring at the Legos.

"Did you pick one?" Nate asked his son.

"The Frost Beast," Cody said, pointing to the toy he wanted.

Nate took it down from the shelf and handed it to him. "You have your money?"

Cody pulled a crinkled wad of bills from his shorts pocket and showed him.

"Let's pay for it and get you to your mom's," he said, then turned to Caitie. "We have to go."

"Nice to meet you, Cody," she said, and he waved goodbye as they walked away. Caitie expelled a huge but silent sigh of relief. Thankfully, by the time she took her items to the register, Nate and his son were gone.

She knew that he had a son, but knowing that and actually seeing them together were two very different things. Knowing he had someone special in his life left her emotions in a ragged, messy jumble, too.

She paid for her things and walked back to her mom's car. As she was getting in, she happened to glance across the street and noticed Nate and Cody standing on the sidewalk outside the pharmacy, chatting with a fresh-faced young woman. Cody was bent over a stroller by her side, playing with the infant in the seat.

Could that be Nate's "special" friend? Caitie was too far away to see clearly, but she could tell that the woman was very pretty. And very young.

Too young for him anyway.

The girl must have said something witty, because first he smiled, and then he broke out laughing. Caitie felt a tug of something unpleasant and for one instant of pure insanity longed to have him smile at her that way, to laugh at one of her clever quips. Touch her arm affectionately...

As if he sensed her gaze, Nate looked in Caitie's direction and caught her staring. The tips of her ears burned with embarrassment, and though her first instinct was to look away, she held her head high and nodded cordially as she climbed into her mom's car. She chanced a peek in her rearview mirror as she drove away, feeling a deep shaft of disappointment when she realized he wasn't watching her longingly. And why would he with a pretty young blonde vying for his attention?

Why did she even care? She wasn't planning to stay here. As soon as she got a job offer she would be back in New York. Back to her *real* life.

Caitie forced herself to look away and headed home. Her mom, who had complained of a headache after dinner, was already in bed, and it was too late to start working in the yard. Cait parked herself in front of the television in the den, feeling edgy and unsettled for no good reason. She was still awake and watching a *Law & Order* rerun when her dad got home at midnight.

"Rough day?" he asked when he poked his head in the den to say good-night, the scent of the food he'd been cooking all day embedded in his clothes.

She sighed and said, "You have no idea."

"Anything I can do to help?"

She shook her head. She wished there were something he could do, but she was a grown woman. She needed to figure this out on her own.

"I hate seeing you so unhappy." he said, looking troubled.

"I'm not unhappy. I guess I just feel as if I'm in flux. But everything will be better when I find a job and get back to New York."

"A good night's sleep will make things clearer."

He was probably right, but when she climbed into bed an hour later, sleep wouldn't come. Her body was exhausted, but her mind was moving a million miles an hour.

She dozed off sometime after two and woke at eight-fifteen with a blazing headache, feeling no less confused than she had been last night. She contemplated going back to sleep—and maybe staying asleep until it was time to go back to New York, but the scent of coffee coerced her out from under the covers.

She pulled a robe on over the oversize shirt she slept in and tried to finger-comb the tangles from her hair. When that proved futile, she grabbed a hair tie off the bedside table and pulled her unruly locks back into a messy ponytail instead.

On a typical day her dad would be out the door and on his way to the diner by 5:30 a.m., but when she shuffled into the kitchen he was seated at the table, drinking coffee and reading the paper. Her mom stood at the stove making pancakes, and thick-sliced pepper bacon sizzled on the griddle.

"Playing hooky?" Caitie asked, kissing his balding head.

He looked up from his paper and smiled. "I take two days a week off now."

"Really?"

"And he never works longer than a ten-hour shift," her mom said cheerfully. The long hours he worked, and his refusal to hire more help, had always been a source of friction between them.

Caitie poured herself a cup of coffee, then slid into the seat beside his, which had always been "her" regular spot. "How do you manage that?"

"I told you about Curtis," her mom said, flipping the pancakes onto a plate she had warmed in the oven, cursing when she flipped a little too hard and one landed on the floor.

"Not that I recall," Caitie said.

"Sure I did. He's our assistant manager." She set the serving plate of pancakes and bacon on the table, then she opened the side door and tossed the runaway pancake into the yard for the birds.

Caitie shrugged. "Not ringing a bell."

"We hired him…how long ago, Lou?"

"Two months ago," her dad said, helping himself to three pancakes and two slices of bacon.

"Mom, I definitely would have remembered that."

"Eat something," her mom said, grabbing a plate from the cupboard and setting it in front of her. "If you lose any more weight, you'll disappear."

Her mom piled two pancakes and four slices of bacon on her plate. Feeling her arteries constrict from the potential saturated animal fat, she put two slices back on the serving plate. "I'm not very hungry."

"What are you up to today?" her dad asked.

"Actually, I had an idea that I wanted to run past you guys," Caitie said. "How would you feel if I used my time off to do some sprucing up in the yard?"

Her mom blushed with embarrassment. "It looks awful out there, I know. It shames me every time someone comes over."

"You don't like to garden anymore?"

"No, I still love it, but it's these darned headaches holding me back. Intense sunlight will almost always trigger a migraine. I'm limited to working outside late in the evening just before dusk, but I'm so tired by then."

"Well, if it's okay with you and Dad, I'd like to remove all the landscaping from the flower beds and redesign it all. Something that will look pretty but be easier to take care of. I also want to talk to someone about painting the house. It needs it, but it's not a job I think I can handle on my own."

He mom looked more troubled than excited. "How much will all this cost?"

"I'm not sure. Why? Are you having money problems? Are things bad at the diner?" They knew they could come to Caitie if they were having financial difficulties. There had been a few times in the past, during the worst part of the recession, when Caitie had helped them cover Kelly's tuition. She had the money and was happy to do it, despite feeling as if it was a bit like flushing her money down the toilet. Kelly was three years in and had already changed her major a dozen times. She didn't seem to have a clue as to what she wanted to do with her life, aside from finding a rich husband to take care of her.

A lofty goal for someone like Caitie, but Kelly would probably pull it off. She had a way of always getting exactly what she wanted, especially with guys. They flocked around her, tripping over themselves to get her attention. She could probably have any man she wanted.

"Things are fine at the diner," her mom assured her. "We just have a few added expenses and things are a little tight."

"Then I'll pay for the home improvements."

"You're here to *save* money," her dad said sternly.

"Consider it my gift to you both for taking me in."

"Oh, honey. You don't owe us anything," her mom said. "There will *always* be a place here for you."

"I know, but I really want to do this for you guys."

"You don't *have* to do anything while you're here," her dad said. "Relax. Take a break. Read a book—hang out with old friends."

"Dad, if I don't find something constructive to do here, I'll crawl out of my skin. I'm used to working sixteen-hour days. I have to keep busy." It would also give her the perfect excuse to avoid town. Which meant avoiding Nate.

"She never was one to be idle," Cait's mom reminded him. "A trait she gets from her father, I think."

He sighed with defeat. "I don't like the idea of you using your own money. But if it's what you really want…"

"It is." Caitie bolted up from her chair to hug him. "Thanks, Dad. I was thinking I might drive to Denver today for supplies. I'll have to borrow Mom's car, since mine is…" She trailed off, dread pooling in her belly as she looked at the clock and saw that it was almost eight-thirty. *Oh no.* She couldn't have!

Bile rose in her throat and she thought for a second that her coffee was going to make a repeat performance. "Please tell me that clock is wrong."

Her dad confirmed the time on his cell phone. "Looks right to me."

Muttering a curse, Caitie slumped in her chair and dropped her head in her hands. How the hell could she have done this?

Concern in her voice, her mom asked, "What's the matter, Caitie?"

Caitie prided herself on her keen memory. She still recalled word for word conversations she'd had as far back as grade school. So how could she have forgotten something this important? A *promise*. She didn't break promises. "I am so screwed."

She reminded her parents about the police report she was supposed to go fill out this morning. Instead it had completely slipped her mind.

"What am I going to do?" she said, looking from her mom to her dad, hoping they had an answer for her. A way to fix this.

"If I were you," her mom said, getting up to clear the table, "I would start with the truth."

What if Nate didn't want to hear the truth? He would never believe that she hadn't blown him off intentionally. Hell, if she were him, *she* probably wouldn't believe her, either. Was she unconsciously trying to sabotage any chance of him not hating her guts?

"Does it really matter to you what Nate thinks?" her dad asked.

It shouldn't have. It wasn't *supposed* to. She had nothing to prove to him. But the people pleaser in her hated letting anyone down.

Her mom set the dishes in the sink and glanced out

the window. "Whatever you say, you had better come up with something fast."

Cait's heart took a dive. "Why?"

"Nate just pulled into the driveway."

Chapter Five

Feeling duped, Nate parked his cruiser in the Cavanaughs' driveway and killed the engine, so hot under the collar his neck burned. Caitie had better be unconscious or dead. Those were the only excuses he could possibly accept for her blowing off their appointment this morning. He'd given her the benefit of the doubt and like a fool hung around the station until almost eight-thirty waiting for her to show.

He had given Caitie the perfect opportunity to redeem herself. All she had to do was show up. Instead she had taken the olive branch he'd offered and thrown it back in his face. Confirming to him yet again that she wasn't the person she used to be. And by believing otherwise, he'd only set himself up to be disappointed.

From the passenger's seat he snatched the file that Caitie had left in his car yesterday. After he returned it, he was washing his hands of the entire situation. As far as he was concerned, after today, Caitie didn't exist.

He angled out of the car into the dusty heat and walked to the back porch. Betty must have seen him coming because as he climbed the wood steps she opened the storm door.

"Hi there, Deputy," she said with a smile. When he was in uniform she always addressed him by his rank. In plainclothes he was always Nate.

It had been awkward, after almost a year of calling them Mom and Dad, to begin addressing Cait's parents by their names. At first he had tried using Mr. and Mrs. Cavanaugh, or sir and ma'am, but they didn't like that. Too formal, Lou had said. So Nate had taken to calling them Lou and Betty.

As he stepped into the kitchen, a wave of familiarity and a deep feeling of loss washed over him. He'd had so many good memories here. Family dinners on Sundays. Scrabble and Trivial Pursuit marathons with her parents, and the occasional penny-ante poker game.

There were unpleasant memories, too. Like the day he'd sat at the kitchen table, Cait's parents trying to console him. And when they had refused to tell him where she went, or why she left in the first place, he'd felt betrayed not just by Caitie, but them, as well. Only after he became a parent did he understand that Lou and Betty were just protecting their child. As any good parent would.

To Nate it was as if she'd vanished, and at the time, their refusal to help him roused suspicions of something dark and sinister. How well did he really know her parents? What if there had been some terrible accident—or maybe it hadn't been an accident at all—and her body was resting in a shallow grave somewhere in the yard? At the time it had seemed the only logical explanation, or the only one he could wrap his head around. Because *his* Caitie would never up and leave without a word.

Then he got the letter. It was postmarked from New York, the address penned in Cait's neat and precise handwriting.

Her pathetic excuse for an apology.

She hadn't even had the decency to tell him *why* she left, when as far as he knew she had planned to go to school in Denver. He still didn't know. The difference now was that he no longer gave a damn. That's what he kept telling himself. But if he was genuinely over it, what was he doing here?

"Your daughter around?" he asked Betty when what he should have done was turn and walk away.

She opened the door to let him in. "If you're referring to my eldest, she's upstairs."

"Thanks." He headed for the stairs.

"Nate, wait!" she called, but he was already three-quarters of the way up by the time she reached the bottom step.

Below him he heard her sigh, then mumble something about "kids." But that was the problem: they *weren't* kids anymore.

He banged on the door of the room that Caitie had shared with her sister and from inside heard her say, "Hold on, I'll be right—"

He flung the door open…and froze. His eyes settled on the smooth, pale skin of Cait's bare midsection as she tugged her shirt on. She was so thin, he could see her ribs. And was that the edge of a black lace bra…?

Like the blade of a dull knife, a jab of desire impaled him, so vivid and disorienting he couldn't move. Not even to peel his eyes away.

Her hair was in a messy ponytail. Her cheeks had a hollowed-out look that only accentuated the dark circles under her eyes. She looked like hell. So why on earth could he think of nothing but putting his hands all over her?

"I can see that you're mad at me, but I can explain," she said, and as quickly as the lusty urges had gripped him, his anger tamped them back under the surface.

"Can you?" he said, both wanting and resenting her simultaneously.

"It's not what you think."

He folded his arms over his chest. "Were you being held against your will?"

She blinked. "Um, no."

"Were you in a coma? *Unconscious?*"

"Just exhausted and stressed out."

Aren't we all. "Yet capable of dialing a phone."

"Yes, but—"

"That's what I thought. Here you go." He handed her the folder, and before she could get another word out, he was pounding back down the stairs. He wasn't surprised to hear the much softer thud of Cait's footsteps behind him.

She caught up with him at the back porch. "Come on, Nate."

"You mean Deputy," he said over his shoulder as he walked to his car. She had given up the privilege of using his first name.

"Would you please just listen to me? I feel guilty enough as it is."

He doubted that.

"Nate, I'm so sorry. I really meant to be there. I just…forgot. I slept in."

He wasn't buying it. He pulled open the driver's side door and said, "You never forget things."

Something in her tone changed. "Nate, do you have the slightest idea what I've been going through? The stress I've been under?"

Not his problem, but as he turned to get into the car, he made the monumental mistake of looking at her. Tears swam in her eyes and she looked so miserable, so sick with guilt, he could feel his anger tick down a notch or two.

"Could you cut me at least a *little* slack?" she said. "I haven't been myself. If I were, I would *not* have forgotten to meet you."

Hard as he tried to cling to his anger, some of it leaked away. Maybe it *had* been an honest mistake.

"If you give me a minute to do something with my hair, I'll go to the station right now," she said. "Lock me in the back of your car again if you don't trust me."

The only reason he insisted on doing a report in the first place is that she didn't want to. Which he couldn't deny was childish of him. Was it really worth it to continue to pursue this when the point was totally lost on her?

"Forget about the report," he said.

Her head tilted. "Are you sure? I really don't mind going. I *want* to go."

"Just…forget it."

She eyed him warily, as if this were some sort of trick. "You're *sure?*"

"Just promise me one thing. The next time your car

stalls in an intersection, don't try to move it by yourself. Call for help and wait for the tow. You could have hurt yourself or someone else."

"People were getting irritated with me. I don't like to inconvenience anyone. I thought I could do it myself. But since the car in question is going to the junkyard, that won't be an issue again."

He should have left it at that, climbed in his car and driven away. Instead he heard himself say, "I'm surprised no one stopped to help you."

"I'm not. I'm a stranger to a good majority of the town now, and no one would remember my car after all these years. I'm sure if someone had recognized me, they would have stopped."

"Or maybe they did recognize you," he said, steeling himself against the brief but very real hurt look that flashed across her face. But it was no use; he felt like a jerk anyway. It wasn't in his nature to be cruel or unkind or to abuse his authority. He got into this career to help people. Not harass them.

Caitie seemed to bring out the worst in him.

"You know, we don't have to be enemies," she said.

"Well, I don't want to be your friend, either. So what else is there?"

She chewed her lip for a second, then brightened and said, "Frenemies?"

He nearly cracked a smile. "That's not even a real word."

"I'm pretty sure it is."

"Nope. I took a lot of psychology courses. There's no such thing as frenemies."

"You wanted to be a psychologist?"

"It's required for the FBI."

Her brows rose. "You applied to the *FBI?* Seriously?"

"I was thinking about it, but I decided to stay here instead."

"Here? Where nothing ever happens? Interesting career move."

Nate shrugged and said, "Least I have a career."

"Oh, *ouch*. Awesome comeback."

The corners of his lips tilted upward. "You're making it very easy."

Eye's lowered, she said, "I'm sorry. I don't know why I'm being so snotty."

"You might want to try that again," he said. "This time with a little eye contact. Like you mean it."

She smiled, looked him directly in the eye and said, "I'm sorry, Deputy."

When he told her to call him that, he never dreamed how annoying it would be. And she looked so much like the Caitie from seven years ago, *his* Caitie, it would have been perfectly natural to pull her close and kiss her. Instead he climbed into the cruiser and started the engine. Before he pulled away, he leaned out the window and said, "Maybe it would be best if we just avoided each other."

"That works for me," Caitie said. "I would never want to risk coming between you and your girlfriend."

He wasn't sure who she was talking about, since he was currently unattached, but he took the ball and ran with it. "I appreciate that."

For several seconds, there was an awkward silence, as if neither was sure what to say or do next, and when they finally did think of something, they ended up talking over one another. They just couldn't seem to get in sync.

"Sorry," Caitie said. "You go first."

"I have to get back to work," he said, and she looked relieved. "I apologize for barging in uninvited while you..."

She shrugged and waved it off. "It's nothing you haven't seen before."

No, he could say with complete confidence that he had never seen her wear a black lace bra, and the vision seemed to have emblazoned itself onto his brain.

A bass-heavy pop song began to play and Caitie reached into the back pocket of her cut-off jean shorts for her phone. She checked the screen and he could swear he actually saw her heart jump in her chest. "I have to take this."

They had said all there was to say anyway. "I'll see you around."

She almost smiled, and Nate found himself wishing she would. "See you around."

She walked toward the house, and he forced himself to look anywhere but her denim-encased behind.

So this is it, he thought as he drove away. She had popped into his life, then right back out again. He knew it was for the best, so why, as he drove back into town, did he feel so lousy? They'd barely gotten reacquainted, yet for some ridiculous reason, Nate felt as if he was losing her all over again.

When Caitie saw Mark Davis, her headhunter's name, on the caller ID, her heart slammed to the pit of her stomach, then rose up to lodge next to her tonsils. Suddenly the situation with Nate seemed slightly less critical. Had Mark gotten her an interview? Was she practically on her way home?

She answered and after exchanging brief pleasantries, Mark got right to the point. "With the investigation heating up, no reputable firm will even look at your résumé."

Damn. "How is it heating up?"

"Don't you watch the news?"

"I've been busy."

"They found the CFO," he told her. Then he added, "Well, what was left of him."

Oh, God.

She slapped a hand over her mouth, feeling as if she might be sick. She didn't actually know the CFO very well, and yes, he had questionable morals, but he didn't deserve to die.

"The point is, until the situation settles down, if I were you, I would lay low for a while."

That was absolutely the last thing she wanted to hear. When it came to headhunters, Mark was at the top of his game. If he couldn't find her a job, there were none to be had. "What am I supposed to do now?"

"Expand your search."

"To other cities?"

"Chicago, Los Angeles…you could even look abroad."

But she liked New York. She felt at home there. A different country sounded exciting, but with her parents getting older, she wouldn't want to be so far away. "Let's exhaust our efforts domestically before we start thinking global."

"Any place in particular that you absolutely wouldn't want to live?"

"In the U.S.?" Other than Paradise? "Nothing comes to mind."

"Okay. I'll get right to work on it."

After they hung up, Caitie opened the storm door and stepped into the kitchen. Her dad was upstairs showering, and her mom was loading the dishwasher.

"Is everything okay between you and Nate?" her mom asked.

"Probably about as good as it'll ever be. It's my headhunter who had the really bad news." Caitie told her about the call.

"I could be here awhile. If you don't mind me staying, that is."

"Oh, honey," her mom said, and gave Caitie a big warm hug. Nothing beat a mom hug at a time like this. "Stay as long as you need to. Things will get better. I promise. We all go through hardships. Those are the times we build the most character."

Caitie couldn't help thinking she was partially to blame for this. She should have seen the illegal activity going on around her. Or maybe she didn't *want* to see.

At any rate, in the future—*if* anyone would ever hire her again—she would be a lot less likely to indiscriminately trust the people she worked for or with. And at times like this, the thought of leaving the rat race for a slower-paced career held surprising allure. But the cost of living was so inflated in the Big Apple, without a high-paying corporate job she would be stuck forever in her tiny studio apartment.

"Your sister called while you were outside," her mom said, and Caitie smothered a groan. "She said to say hi."

Cait rolled her eyes. She couldn't help it. When was

the last time Kelly had picked up the phone and called Caitie? Or even sent her an email.

"Oh, honey, don't be like that," her mom said, but she knew as well as Caitie that Kelly was not an easy person to love. She finished loading the dishwasher, poured detergent in the tray and set it to run. "I know she's difficult—"

"*Difficult?*"

"I wish you two could at least try to get along."

Caitie *had* tried, but there was just too much resentment there. Too many hurt feelings. Kelly wasn't even supposed to be born. After a high-risk birth that had nearly killed Caitie and her mom, she was told it would be too much of a risk to have more kids. Her mom had her tubes tied…only to learn four years later that one of the tubes had miraculously *untied* itself and she was pregnant again.

The day they brought the screaming smelly bundle home from the hospital, Caitie went from being the only child to the invisible child. Kelly cried almost nonstop the first three months—or so it had seemed to Caitie. She had vivid memories of following her mom as she paced the house or the yard, trying to calm Kelly, tugging on her mom's shirt, hoping for just a minute or two of her attention.

Despite being a fussy baby, Kelly was gorgeous. With her big blue eyes and wispy hair, she looked like a China doll. People oohed and ahhed over her, always wanting to hold her.

"Your baby is so beautiful!" people would gush. If they even noticed Caitie, which they often didn't, they might smile vaguely and tell her she was pretty, too. Or *cute*. She got that one a lot. But Kelly was the main attraction, and she fed on the attention. The more people doted on her, the more she needed. And the less attention Caitie got, the more her resentment grew. Kelly was gorgeous; Caitie was cute. Kelly had droves of friends; Caitie was quiet and shy. Kelly was described as spirited and fun; Caitie was the "smart" one.

When Kelly hit puberty, the real fun began—to this day, Caitie was still convinced Kelly had been a victim of demonic possession. She was always pushing the boundaries of the rules set for them by their parents and her teachers. As if they were not actu[...] rules, but guidelines she could choose to ignore if she so desired. Which she often did. As far as Kelly was concerned, she stood at the center of existence and the universe revolved around her.

"Kelly does love you," her mom said.

"Kelly loves Kelly."

"Yes, but she's trying." She rung out a dishrag and wiped off the table and chairs. "Your dad and I are just happy that she's in school."

"You realize that the University of Southern California was ranked one of the top party schools in the nation by a certain gentlemen's publication? It's the only reason she wanted to go there."

"At least she's there." Her mom rinsed the rag then folded it neatly and draped it over the faucet.

"What you mean is, she's not *here* driving you crazy."

Her mom sighed and turned to Caitie, looking exhausted. Kelly often had that effect on people. "I love your sister."

"You can love someone but not like them very much," Caitie told her. "I can attest to that."

Not that she wished her sister ill will; she was just happier keeping her at a comfortable distance. Twenty-five hundred miles, give or take.

"I know there are hard feelings between you two," her mom said. "I realize she got more attention. But you know what they say about the squeaky wheel. In many ways, you were a self-regulating teenager."

"Self-regulating?"

She untied her apron—the same one she'd used since Caitie was little—and hung it on a hook in the broom closet. "We never had to worry about you getting into trouble or neglecting your schoolwork. If we said be home at eleven, you were usually five or ten minutes early. If we asked you to do something, you didn't ask why or complain that you didn't have time. Whether it was chores around the house or working weekends at the diner, you just did it, no questions asked."

Caitie could count on two hands how many times Kelly had helped out in the diner, and it was always under duress. She *hated* it there.

"I'm sorry that we didn't tell you more often how much we appreciated you," her mom said, and Caitie felt a jab of guilt.

"I know you did." She gave her mom a hug, squeezing extra hard. "And I knew it back then, too. Hell, my friends would have *loved* the kind of independence I had. Mel used to get so jealous. I don't know if you remember how strict her parents were with her and her little brother."

"I remember."

And super critical. Mel's mom placed too much value on appearances. She had always been after Mel

about her weight, putting her on one diet after another, forcing her to participate in the latest exercise craze. But nothing ever seemed to work. Not long-term anyway. And it wasn't as if Mel gorged herself or ate unhealthy foods. As Mel had put it, she had the metabolism of a turtle. She could eat carrot sticks and celery for a month and still manage to gain a pound or two.

Caitie hadn't thought much of it at the time, but looking back, all that criticism must have been devastating for Mel. Especially when her brother Pete was the golden child.

"Do you think I did the right thing when I left?" Caitie asked her. "Because I can't help feeling like a coward."

Her mom blinked with surprise. "A *coward?* Caitie, honey, you are one of the bravest, not to mention smartest, people I know. And I'm not just saying that because you're my daughter. You left. As difficult as it was, and as conflicted as you felt, you followed your dream. You moved to a city where you had never been and didn't know a single soul. That took tremendous courage. More than I ever had."

"The way I left wasn't very courageous."

"Caitie, you did what you had to do. Imagine the alternative. What if you had stayed, if you had married Nate. Where do you think you would be right now?"

It wouldn't be domestic bliss; that was for sure. Or would it have been?

"Other than alienating your friends, do you have any regrets about leaving?"

Caitie gave that one some thought. Even with the investigation, and the demise of her career looming, leaving had been the right thing to do. "No, I don't."

"Then wouldn't you say that you made the right choice?"

She was using that Vulcan logic again. But this time Caitie didn't mind so much. "I guess so."

Her mom looked at her watch. "If you're going to drive all the way to Denver, you should get moving."

"You're sure you don't mind me taking your car?"

"Not at all. But will you have room for everything?"

Ugh. She hadn't considered that. She'd forgotten what a pain it could be living in the boonies. "Do you think dad would let me take the work van?"

Once a month for as long as Caitie could remember, her parents drove to the Restaurant Supply in Denver and came home with the back of the utility van packed floor to ceiling. She recalled those occasions vividly, because from the time she was twelve, whenever her parents went to the city, they left Caitie in charge of her sister, who hounded her constantly to play Barbies or color or watch cartoons. It was always me, me, me.

"Of course I'll let you take it," her dad said as he walked into the kitchen holding an empty coffee cup. His hair—what was left of it—was damp and combed back neatly. Her dad had worn his hair long until it began thinning in his thirties—after Kelly was born, of course. Caitie had vivid memories of playing with it. He'd let her braid it or roll it up into her mom's curlers.

She kissed her dad's cheek. "Thanks, Dad."

She was on the road an hour later, chugging down the highway, window down, a warm breeze blowing through her hair while her favorite Bruno Mars CD played "Just The Way You Are." The farther she

drove, the more relaxed she began to feel. So relaxed that when she reached the turnoff for Denver, she almost kept going.

Chapter Six

It was nearly midnight when Caitie rolled back into town, the rear of the van stuffed with everything she would need for the landscape face-lift. Paradise was dark and tucked into bed for the night, Main Street all but deserted. As she passed the diner, she happened to glance over, and could see through the front window that a heat lamp had been left on in the kitchen. Her dad would have never forgotten something like that, but he hadn't worked today, so this one was on the new assistant manager.

She was up about two hours past her usual bedtime, and all she wanted to do was crawl under the covers and sleep off the headache that had begun to beat relentlessly in her temples about halfway home. She doubted the light could be hot enough to start a

fire, but why take chances? Plus, it was a waste of electricity.

With a sigh of exhaustion, she turned left down a side street and doubled back, cutting through the alley behind the dentist's office next door. She parked just outside the diner's rear entrance.

She shut the van off and climbed out, diner key in hand, but when she touched the doorknob to unlock it, the door pushed open on its own.

Caitie yanked her hand away and stepped back in alarm, as if the knob had burned her. It was possible that the assistant manager could have accidentally left it unlocked—which, coupled with leaving the light on, didn't bode well for the guy—but what if that wasn't the case? What if someone had broken in? They could *still* be in there.

Heart pounding, she yanked the van door open and leaped in, slamming and locking it behind her. She ducked down in her seat and pulled her phone out of her purse. Knowing a cellular call could bounce around half a dozen counties before it made it to the right place, she dialed the police station directly, thankful she kept the number in her phone.

"We'll get someone over there ASAP," the dispatch told her, and, boy, he wasn't kidding. Not three minutes later a police car pulled up behind the van, but when the officer climbed out and she saw who it was in the mirror, she groaned.

Seriously?

She pushed the door open and hopped out.

Nate didn't look any less annoyed to see her. "What seems to be the problem...*ma'am?*"

"I thought you work days...*Deputy.*"

Sounding impatient, he said, "You reported a possible break-in?"

"I noticed a heat lamp on as I was driving by. I was going to go in and shut it off, but when I came back here to unlock the door, it was already open."

"Is anything missing?"

She shrugged. "How should I know?"

"You haven't been inside?"

"Of course not! What if whoever broke in is still in there?"

"This isn't New York City," Nate said with a look that suggested she was a total moron for even considering there could be any foul play. "Someone probably forgot to lock up. It's more plausible than a break-in."

There hadn't been a murder in Paradise since the fifties, but it was bound to happen again someday. She'd prefer it not be her mutilated, decomposing corpse that broke the cycle.

"What kind of person would break into the diner?" Nate asked her.

"A hungry one?"

He folded his arms, gave her that look.

"Could you just check. *Please?* It is your job, right?"

Looking less than enthused, he sighed heavily and said, "If it will make you feel better."

"It will. Thank you."

One hand resting casually on his firearm, Nate strolled into the diner as if he were going in for a late supper, not to catch a possible intruder. She stood outside the door, leaning in to listen for the sound of a scuffle. It was almost *too* quiet.

Maybe she was being overly cautious, but when it came to her personal safety, a woman could never be too careful. She'd learned that lesson the hard way when her purse was snatched right off her shoulder in the middle of the afternoon on a busy city street. By the time she got home and called the credit card company to cancel her card, the snatcher had used it all over Manhattan.

Nate reappeared barely a minute later. There was no way he'd had time to check the *entire* restaurant.

"No one in there?" she asked.

"No, there's someone here," he said, and her breath hitched.

He summoned her to follow him. Had he subdued the guilty party, and if he had, wouldn't she have heard something?

Heart in her throat, she followed him to the office. There at the desk, head resting on the blotter, sound asleep, sat her dad.

"There's your intruder," Nate whispered, sounding smug. "Should I alert SWAT?"

She glared at him.

He glared back. Then almost…smiled?

"Dad?" Caitie said, touching his shoulder.

He shot upright, blinking himself awake, rubbing the sleep from his eyes. He looked at his watch. "Caitie, honey, what are you doing here so late? And why is Nate here?"

"I was on my way back from Denver and I saw that a heat lamp was still on. I was going to turn it off. When I found the door unlocked, I was worried someone broke in. I called the police."

He rubbed his eyes with the heels of his palms. "I'm sorry if I scared you."

"How did you get here? I didn't see your car."

"Mom was parked behind me at home so I took her car. The alley was full when I got here, so I parked on the side street."

"Why are you here so late?"

"Your mom went to bed early, so I came in to catch up on some paperwork. I haven't quite figured out her system. Computers were never my thing."

"Why don't you ask Mom to help you?"

Her dad hesitated, looked from Caitie to Nate, then said, "That's something we should probably talk about."

"She doesn't know?" Nate asked, and Lou shook his head.

Cait's heart sank so hard and fast it left a painful void in her chest. "What don't I know?"

"I know this is none of my business, but you need to tell her," Nate said.

"Yes, please, tell me," she said to her dad, annoyed that Nate knew what was going on when she hadn't the slightest clue.

"Since there's no trouble here, I'm going to go," Nate said.

Caitie turned to him. "Thank you for your help."

He shrugged. "I didn't do much."

"I think the correct response would be, 'You're welcome,'" she said, and she could swear that he nearly smiled.

"You're welcome."

When he was gone, Caitie asked her dad, "Is something wrong with Mom?"

"You've probably noticed that your mom's memory isn't so great anymore."

She sat on the edge of the desk. "I figured it was the migraine pills. She said they make her loopy."

"That's what we thought it was at first, too."

"But it's not?"

He shook his head solemnly, and Cait's heart plummeted, her first thought of course being cancer. Her paternal grandfather had been diagnosed with pancreatic cancer when Caitie was in middle school. They had spent the following six months watching him waste away. The thought of her mom going through that…

Her dad reached out and touched her arm and her heart sank even lower, till she could feel it pounding all the way in the pit of her stomach. "Honey, your mom was diagnosed with Alzheimer's."

"*Alzheimer's?* How is that possible? She's not even fifty!"

"She has early-onset Alzheimer's."

The fast-food burger she'd had for dinner backed up in Caitie's throat. Deep down she had known that something wasn't right, but she had never imagined it could be this bad. "When did this happen?"

"We started to really notice changes about six months ago. Little things, like your mom forgetting where she put her reading glasses, or forgetting a customer's drink. She laughed it off as old age. But then she started forgetting appointments and to pay some of the bills. Last month she drove to Denver for restaurant supplies. I didn't want her going alone, but she insisted she was fine. She called me later that day in a panic. She couldn't remember how to get home. I took her to the doctor the very next day. They sent her to a specialist in Denver."

Only when he took her hand did she realize it was

balled up tight and her fingernails were cutting painfully into her palm. "Does Kelly know?"

He shook his head. "Your mother wanted to tell you in person. When the time was right."

"If you had told me about her diagnosis, I could have at least been helping," Caitie told him.

"With everything going on in your life, we didn't want to bother you with it."

"*Bother* me? I'm your child, for God's sake! You know, the daughter who actually gives a damn."

"You had enough to deal with in New York. Besides, your mom and I have been through rough times before. We'll get through this."

He said that as if at some point she would be cured. Cait knew very little of the disease, but the one thing she did know was that it was fatal.

No wonder they'd hired a manager. Her poor dad must have been running himself ragged dealing with the restaurant by himself, plus taking care of her mom.

"While I'm in Paradise, why don't you let me take over the accounting and the ordering?" Caitie said. That would take at least a little bit of the burden from his shoulders.

She half expected him to argue with her, but instead he looked relieved. "Well, if you wouldn't mind. We'll pay you."

"Consider it my rent."

"Caitie—"

"You're not going to win this one, so don't even try," she said. Cait's mom had worked so hard all her life, had done so many wonderful things for her friends and the community. She didn't deserve this.

"Are you okay?" he asked.

Nope. She was nowhere close to okay, but an emotional meltdown was out of the question. Her dad needed her to be strong. "I do have one question. Why is it that my ex-boyfriend knew about this before I did?"

"All the local law enforcement knows. So if they should find her wandering aimlessly down Main Street, unsure of how to get home, they'll know what to do. They keep an eye on her for me. But at some point she'll need care 24/7."

It still irked her, but she was happy to know that someone was looking out for her mom. "Who else knows?"

"Only her doctor and her cousin in Boulder. She's afraid that when people learn the truth, they'll treat her differently, but I'm not sure if she'll be able to keep it secret for much longer. People are beginning to talk."

That set Caitie's nerves on edge. "It's no one else's business."

"Small towns," he said with a shrug, as if it didn't bother him one bit. "I have an entire police force looking out for my wife at all times. There's not a big-city police department in the world that would do that."

He was right.

Her dad looked at his watch, then patted her hand. "It's late. Go home, get a good night's rest and we'll talk about this tomorrow, okay?"

She nodded. Though her mind was in overdrive, exhaustion seeped from her pores. She just wanted to curl up and fall asleep and pretend this whole conversation was just a bad dream and her mom wasn't dying.

"Are you coming, too?" she asked her dad. "You want me to wait?"

"Go ahead. I'll just be a few minutes behind you."

She walked out the back door, furious at the world, at the unfairness of it all. She tugged the van keys from her pocket, nearly stumbling over her own feet when she looked up and realized Nate's cruiser was still parked there. He stood by the van, arms folded, leaning against the driver's side door.

Would this hellish day never end?

"You lost?" she asked him.

She braced herself for a snotty comeback, for him to put her in her place. Welcomed it even, because anger was such an easy emotion. Better that than face how she was really feeling, to accept that life as she knew it had been forever altered.

Nate took a step toward her. *Bring it on,* she thought, bracing herself for a well-deserved tongue-lashing. Instead he reached out, pulled her into his arms and held her. "I'm sorry, Caitie."

Sorry? How did he expect her to respond? Did he honestly believe that she would go all gooey and melt into his arms? She searched inside herself for the will—the *strength*—to push him away. She could handle this herself. She didn't need him of all people to lean on.

She flattened her hands against his chest to push him away, but her fingers curled into the fabric of his shirt and she found herself pulling him closer instead. It was wonderful and awful.

In this crazy, mixed-up disaster that was now her life, in that very instant, he was the only thing that felt real. The heat of his body, the whisper of his breath against her hair drew her in closer when she should have been backing away. It wasn't supposed to be this way. He wasn't supposed to be *nice* to her.

And *she* wasn't supposed to *want* him.

When the call had gone out from dispatch about a possible break-in at the diner, Nate could have easily let the other officer on patrol take it. Yet before he knew what he was doing, the radio was in his hand.

Temporary insanity?

It had to be. He had no business getting himself tangled up in Caitie's problems. Yet here he was, holding her, as she molded herself closer to his body, clung to him. He closed his eyes, breathed in the scent of her hair, her skin. There was a tightness in his chest, a dull ache in the center of his heart.

What the hell was he supposed to do now? Let go and pretend he didn't want to nibble the delicate shell of her ear, or trail kisses down the long, slender column of her neck? Slant his mouth over hers and feed on the sweetness of her mouth, the softness of her lips?

Two days ago everything had been *normal.* Then in came Caitie, thrusting his quiet, meticulously constructed life into total chaos. Much the way she had in high school.

Nate had known Caitie his whole life, but he'd never thought of her in a romantic way when they were kids. The truth was, he never thought of her much at all. She was a brain; he was a jock. She took all college prep courses; he was an average student. He'd passed her in the school hallways and seen her on the sidelines in her cheerleader's uniform, but they had never really spoken.

That changed in their senior year. He had been in

danger of failing math, so he'd signed up for the tutoring program and had been paired with Caitie. She was different than any of the girls he dated. Mature, intelligent, driven. And totally unaware of how beautiful she was.

He would never forget the first time they had kissed. They were in his bedroom, studying for a quiz. He was on the floor, leaning against the bed, while she lay on her stomach on the mattress, propped up on her elbows looking over his shoulder. He happened to notice that she had an eyelash on her cheek, and he reached up to brush it away. He would never forget the way her breath hitched and her pupils dilated. He knew he wanted to kiss her—*had* to kiss her—but Caitie beat him to it. She had been the one to lean in, to press her lips to his. At that point, he took the ball and ran with it. They didn't get much studying done that night, which resulted in a D on the test, but they were inseparable from then on.

It had been so different with Mel. Nate had struggled to be the man—the *husband*—she deserved, to love her with his whole heart, and he'd failed miserably. Now that Caitie was here, he found himself having to hold back, to *stop* feeling.

Why, with Caitie, did it happen so effortlessly? How could something so clearly wrong feel so damned good? So natural.

The back door of the diner swung open, and they swiftly parted, Caitie brushing away what he suspected were tears from her cheeks.

In all the time they'd dated, he'd only seen her cry a handful of times. To the casual observer Caitie seemed quiet, shy and unassuming, when in reality she was tough as nails.

It was obvious to her father that he had interrupted something, but to his credit, Lou pretended not to notice. "Ready to go home?" he asked Caitie.

She sniffled and nodded, turning to Nate. "Thank you."

"Just doing my job," he said, which they both knew was a crock. Something happened to him when Caitie was around. What he used to know about himself, who he was as a man, all seemed backward now. Logically he knew he would be a fool to trust her again, to let himself drop his guard, but his hormones, and his heart, didn't seem to be getting the message.

Maybe Mel was right and he did need closure. Unfortunately, he didn't have the slightest clue how to make that happen.

Chapter Seven

Despite all the tossing and turning she'd done the night before, Caitie rose at dawn the next morning. She sat up in bed with her laptop, researching the early-onset form of Alzheimer's.

It felt like a bad dream. How could something this terrible happen to them? Her mom was a pillar of the community. Despite her busy schedule, she always made time to give back to the town. She had served on the local council for years, and though her own children were out of school locally, she still donated baked goods to the PTA and helped organize the annual PTA yard sale. If she heard that an older resident wasn't well, she would take them a hot meal from the diner, then stay to make sure they actually ate.

Now she would continue to waste away, her memory becoming increasingly worse, until she was the ghost of her former self. Until her body wouldn't even remember how to function. If Caitie went back to New York as planned, her dad would be left to deal with it alone. And when Caitie came back to visit, would her mom even remember her?

The thought broke her heart.

Though she was tempted to pull the covers over her head and wallow in self-pity for the rest of the day, Cait dragged herself out of bed. She found an old pair of denim shorts still in her dresser drawer from high school. As she slipped them over her hips, she was again reminded that she was too thin. She pulled on an old T-shirt and tennis shoes and brushed her hair back into a ponytail.

Heart in her throat, she headed downstairs to the kitchen, expecting to find her mom making breakfast, but the room was dark and quiet. She opened the blinds and saw that her dad's car was already gone.

She put a pot of coffee on to brew, making it extra strong, figuring she could use the added caffeine today. The plan was to spend the day removing everything in the existing flower beds and start over from scratch.

With a steaming cup of coffee in hand, she stepped out onto the back porch. Hot air crowded into her lungs, making it hard to breathe, while sweat beaded her forehead and upper lip. She looked at her cup, wishing it were a tall glass of iced tea instead.

She sipped her coffee as she circled the house, making a mental list of the plants she intended to dig up and save. Until the new beds were ready for planting, she would clear a space in the vegetable patch and use it as a temporary holding garden. The plants, new edging, topsoil and mulch were still in the van, along with all the other supplies she'd purchased.

Allowing herself a brief, sentimental moment, she balanced on one of the railroad ties bordering the beds, the way she had when she was little, knowing without a doubt that if Kelly were there, she wouldn't hesitate to shove Caitie over.

She smiled in spite of herself.

She unloaded the van, building up a sweat as she stacked everything beside the garage. The railroad ties were so deeply planted in the ground, she had to pry them up with a pitchfork, and so old and rotted they came apart like wet papier-mâché. Sweat poured down the sides of her face and neck, soaking her shirt and the cups of her bra. By the time she pulled the last rotted tie from the ground two hours later, she was a sweaty, filthy mess.

"There you are!" she heard her mom say, and turned to see her walking toward Caitie on the wraparound porch. She looked fresh and cool in her yellow-and-white sundress.

Cait's stomach took another sharp dive downward. "Good morning."

"I thought maybe you had left."

"I got an early start," she said, stabbing the pitch-fork into the ground.

"It looks as if you've gotten a lot done."

Yes, but she still had a *long* way to go.

She leaned against the porch rail. "Your dad tells me that you two had a talk last night."

Caitie nodded, her heart sinking in her chest.

Her mom sighed, looking sad. "I'm sorry you had

to find out the way you did. I wanted to tell you myself. To soften the blow."

As if that were even possible. "I can't even imagine what you must be going through," Caitie told her. "I just wish you would have told me sooner. I could have been helping."

"Honey, you have enough to deal with without worrying about me."

Caitie's job and living situation were barely more than a blip on the radar compared to her mom's situation. "As long as I'm here in town, I'll help you with anything you need. Just say the word."

"Do you have any questions?" her mom asked.

"I spent an hour on the internet this morning looking up information."

Her mom smiled. "That doesn't surprise me. You've always dealt with problems head-on."

"I get that from my mom," Cait told her, and she smiled. "You look pretty. Are you going somewhere?"

"I need to make a quick run to the salon and the pharmacy. I don't know if your dad mentioned it, but my doctor thinks I shouldn't be driving."

Her mom had always been such an independent and capable person. How awful it must be for her, having to give that up. "Do you need me to drive you?"

"You wouldn't mind?"

"Of course not," Cait said, peeling her gardening gloves off. "I'm here to help. Just give me a minute to clean up."

She left her dirt-caked shoes on the back porch. When she entered the house, the cool air of the kitchen felt like heaven. She washed her hands and arms in the kitchen sink, then splashed cool water on her face.

She hadn't realized what difficult work this landscaping project would be. Her aching arms and howling lower back said she was already testing the limits of her endurance.

Looking marginally presentable—if one could overlook her dusty, sweat-stained clothes and messy hair—she grabbed her purse, shoved her feet into her flip-flops and headed back outside.

Her mom didn't say much on the drive. She just looked wistfully out the window, watching the landscape roll past.

They went to the pharmacy first, and while her mom was inside picking up prescriptions, Caitie waited in the car out front, earning more than a few curious glances. The ones who recognized her either stopped to say hello or waved. She even got a few "welcome homes."

Her mom came out several minutes later. As she got back in the car Caitie could tell immediately that something was wrong.

"You okay?" she asked.

Her mom frowned, lightly touching her temple. "I feel a headache coming on. I must have forgotten to take my medication this morning."

"Then we should go straight home."

"First we have to stop at the salon. I used the last of my shampoo this morning. It'll just take me a minute."

Caitie pulled back out onto Main Street and drove toward the salon three blocks up, but the closest parking spot she could find was nearly two blocks away. A long way to walk in the bright sunshine with a migraine headache. Considering the way her mom sat with her head back and her eyes closed, pressing her temples with her index fingers, it was shaping up to be a bad one.

"Why don't I run in and grab it for you," Caitie said.

"If you wouldn't mind. Just tell them it's for me. They'll know which kind." She handed Caitie a twenty-dollar bill. "This should cover it."

"I'll be right back." Caitie hopped out and hurried down the sidewalk, head down, dark glasses shading her eyes, aware of how grungy she looked. Had she known she would be getting out of the car, she would have changed her clothes and brushed her hair.

As long as she could remember, the name of the salon had been The Do-Up. But now a new sign hung above the door—Shear Genius—which Caitie had to admit was clever.

The door jingled as she stepped inside. The name wasn't the only thing that had changed. Gone was the yellowing paint, the faded linoleum and outdated equipment. The interior was clean, modern and impressively busy. All but one of the six hair stations and two of the four nail techs had customers. For a small-town salon, they looked to have a thriving clientele.

One of the nail techs, a chubby young woman with fire-red hair, met her at the counter, giving her a subtle once-over, one brow slightly raised. "Can I help you?"

In her grungy clothes, Caitie probably looked more like a vagrant than a paying customer.

"I'm picking up shampoo for my mom," she said. "Betty Cavanaugh. She said you would know which kind."

Recognition and curiosity lit her face. "Oh, you must be Caitie."

"The one and only," she said, hoping to end the conversation there. The girl seemed to take the hint.

She flashed an unnaturally white smile and said, "You just wait right here. I'll go get that from the back."

While she waited, Caitie stood by the front window, her back to the inquisitive, prying eyes and hushed conversations that were no doubt about her.

She caught herself wondering why she hadn't just offered to run the errands herself, so her mom could stay home and rest. Preserve her strength. But hadn't her dad said that she didn't want people treating her differently?

"That'll be eleven fifty-nine," someone said from behind her.

Caitie closed her eyes and cursed under her breath. She knew that voice, and she was so *not* ready for this.

She turned, facing Melanie. Nathan's ex-wife, and Cait's ex-best friend. With her curly auburn hair highlighted and cut in a short, sassy style, she looked young and hip. Not to mention gorgeous. It was no wonder Nate fell for her. Meg may have struggled with her weight, but she was so pretty, with her bright eyes and dimples, those few extra pounds were easy to overlook. Not only that, but Mel was probably one of the genuinely nicest people Caitie had ever known.

Caitie had imagined this scenario a hundred times, always knew exactly what she would say, but now the words couldn't seem to make it from her brain to her mouth.

"Eleven fifty-nine," Mel repeated, as if Caitie were just some random customer off the street. The salon, she realized, had gone dead silent and everyone, customer and employee alike, was shamelessly riveted. Could they have picked a worse place to do this? She knew the instant she walked out the door, cell phones would be buzzing all over the county.

Hands trembling, pulse bouncing erratically in her chest, Caitie walked to the counter where Mel stood and handed her the twenty-dollar bill. The air felt thick with chemicals and tension. Why did she get the feeling this was going to end badly?

Mel rang up the purchase, handed her change over and slid the bottle of shampoo across the counter to her.

Caitie grabbed the bottle, and, though there were so many things she could say to Mel, so many that she wanted to say, she barely managed a mumbled "thank you." She turned and walked to the door, thinking she might just walk away from this unscathed....

"That's it?" Mel said, so loud that the entire shop heard her. "You have nothing else to say to me?"

Caitie cringed. Anything she could say at this point would only add to the tension, so she opened the door; the air outside was a wall of stifling heat.

"Go ahead—walk away," Mel called after her. "That's apparently what you're good at."

Oh, no she didn't....

Caitie spun around to face her. "What's the matter? Were you hoping I may have another boyfriend you could steal? Since you apparently couldn't hold on to the first one."

It was a mean and vindictive thing to say, and Mel's hurt look was more than she could stand. Gathering the remnants of her shredded pride, Cait left the salon and power walked to the car.

Why had she said that? It wasn't like her to be mean and petty. Coming back to Paradise was beginning to feel like a huge mistake.

As she approached the car, she could see her mom in the passenger's seat, talking animatedly on her cell phone. The instant she saw Caitie, she ended the call and tried to look ill, confirming what Caitie had already suspected. There had been no headache, and she had just been set up.

Caitie got in the car and handed the shampoo to her mom, so angry and hurt and humiliated her voice shook. "Is that it?"

She looked at the bottle and nodded. "Yes, this is the right brand. Thank you."

"What I meant was, is there anyone else you'd like me to humiliate myself in front of, or can we go home now?"

If her mom felt the least bit regretful for what she had done, it didn't show. "Let's go home."

Rattled by the encounter, Caitie backed out of the parking space, cutting the wheel too sharply and narrowly missing the car parked beside them.

"Your sister just called," her mom said, as if nothing were amiss. As if Caitie hadn't just endured the second-most humiliating experience of her life. "When I told her that you're here, she said she might come for a visit."

"Wonderful," Caitie grumbled, feeling fed up with the entire world.

"She said she has a surprise."

When Kelly had a *surprise,* all you could do is brace yourself for the impact.

They passed Joe's Place at the end of town, then

turned left down the county road, and she even managed to keep the car out of the ditch this time. She knew she should give herself time to calm down, to vent some of the anger and humiliation clawing at her insides, but she couldn't hold her tongue.

"That was a rotten thing to do to me."

Her mom didn't even try to pretend it was anything other than a ploy to get Caitie and Meg talking again. In a tone that was frustratingly calm and rational, she said, "Don't you think it's about time you two work this out?"

"In front of the *entire* salon? Great idea."

"Caitie—"

"You should have told me she works there. You should have warned me."

"If I had, you wouldn't have gone in, defeating the purpose of this outing. And Mel doesn't just work at the salon. She owns it."

As long as Caitie had known Mel she'd talked about going to cosmetology school. It was all she had ever wanted to do. It made Caitie feel *so* much better to know that Mel was a success, living her dream, while her own career was more or less in the toilet.

Caitie brooded the rest of the way home. Nothing else was said until they were parked in the driveway and getting out of the car.

"You should go back and talk to her," her mom said.

Caitie slammed her door so hard the window shook, and she leveled her eyes on her mom over the roof of the car. "Not going to happen."

"That's what friends do."

"We haven't been friends for a long time. She betrayed me."

"Are you sure about that?"

Caitie blinked. What the heck was that supposed to mean?

"She was your best friend," her mom said.

"*Was.* As in past tense. We haven't talked in seven years."

"And it's time you clear the air. Hear her side of the story before you continue to pass judgment. What she has to say might surprise you."

Chapter Eight

Caitie sat in her mom's car, peering toward the window at Joe's Place down the street. As was typical on a Friday night, the parking lot, and a block's worth of street spaces, were jammed with motorcycles, pickup trucks and a few SUVs and cars in the mix.

It would have been so easy to start the engine and drive back home. Much easier than going inside to face Mel and apologize for what she had said in the salon yesterday. But a brief email update from her headhunter bore little promise of her finding a job anytime soon. Even after widening his search to other major cities, no one was biting. Meaning she would probably be stuck here for a while.

Not to mention that her mom was right. Clearing the air was the right thing to do.

She got out of the car and walked to the bar. Being

the only watering hole in town, Joe's Place had a diverse customer base. She opened the door and stepped inside; the dining room was filled to capacity with couples, groups of young people and families. The other end, near the bar, was standing room only and the jukebox blasted out a twangy country song she'd never heard.

Caitie made her way to the bar, scanning the crowd until she found who she was looking for. She had hoped he wouldn't be here, but there Nate was, sitting at a table by the dance floor with the young girl he'd been talking to on the street the other·day. She looked even younger close up.

Way to rob the cradle, dude.

But that was *none* of her business. She stepped up to the bar and Joe Miller himself was standing there. "Caitlyn Cavanaugh," he said with a grin that made girls swoon. "I heard you were back. I wondered if I would see you in here. You staying long?"

"It's beginning to look that way. I heard you're engaged. Congratulations."

"Thanks." His smile was that of a man who was very happy with his life, and Caitie was glad to see it. Every girl in town had a crush on Joe at one time or another, but he'd only had eyes for Beth, his high school girlfriend. The entire town was stunned when she took off for Los Angeles, leaving Joe to raise their infant daughter alone. According to Cait's mom, the past couple of years had been difficult for him, until he met Reily.

"My fiancée's performing tonight," Joe said.

"That's why I'm here." At least, that was one of the reasons.

"What can I get you?"

She typically stuck to white wine. She'd never been much of a drinker, but tonight she needed something a tad bit stronger. "How about an agave margarita on the rocks with lots of salt on the rim."

"Comin' right up," he said.

She watched him assemble her drink with casual competence; then he set it in front of her on a cocktail napkin. "Six-fifty."

She put a five and three singles down. It was sticker shock but in reverse. The bar she sometimes hung out at near work charged double for the same drink. And Joe's version was ten times better. The perfect blend of agave nectar, tequila, fresh lime juice and soda water. It was diet friendly, too, though the last thing she needed to do was lose more weight.

Someone sidled up beside her and hooked an arm through hers. The perfume she'd bathed herself in gave away the person's identity.

Caitie turned to her, tying not to grimace. "Hey, Zoey."

"Hey back," Zoey said with a plastic smile. She held a half-consumed martini in one hand, and it was clear by the way she listed to one side, then overcompensated as she tried to jerk herself upright, that it was not her first. It seemed she was holding on to Caitie not to be friendly but to keep from falling over.

"The girls and I have a table," she said. "We would love it if you joined us."

For a gossip fest? She couldn't think of a better way to spend her Friday night. *Not.* But was it any worse than hanging out at the bar alone? "Um...sure."

Caitie grabbed her drink and followed Zoey, who

half walked, half stumbled in her spike heels to a table across the dance floor from where Nate and his twinkie—sorry, make that *date*—were sitting. Only they weren't sitting there now. They were on the dance floor, swaying to a slow song, her head resting on his shoulder.

Caitie had an almost overwhelming urge to stomp across the dance floor, rip the girl out of his arms and claw her eyes out. She was so transfixed on Nate that she didn't realize who was sitting at Zoey's table until she was almost of top of it.

Reily was there nursing a beer. Beside her, eyes trained on Caitie, sat Melanie.

Oh boy, here we go again.

"Hi, Caitie!" Reily said, bubbly and warm. "Grab a seat. Do you know Melanie?"

"She knows who I am," Mel said, pinning Caitie with a look that seemed to say, *Sit down. I dare you.* And of course the only empty seat was right next to Mel.

Heart pounding, hands trembling, Caitie slid into the chair. She slammed back half the margarita in one big gulp, wishing she'd told Joe to keep them coming. She also wished she'd gone with her instincts yesterday and kept her mouth shut.

Mel looked amazing in a halter dress the same bluish-green shade as her eyes and strappy sandals that added at least three inches to her petite frame. Her skin glowed and her eyes popped, stirring up old feelings of jealousy in Caitie.

Caitie had always been the "smart" one, while Mel was the "pretty" one. Or that had been the way she had seen it back then. There were times when Caitie would have given anything to switch places with her best friend. Just for a day, to see what it felt like to be so pretty and outgoing, to be liked by so many people. To know exactly what to say and when to say it, without sounding like a total nerd.

When Mel had begged Caitie to join the cheerleading squad with her, Caitie had grudgingly agreed, hoping it might improve her social life. All it did was take up more of her precious free time. She never quite felt she belonged in their clique. There was too much competition and cattiness, too much jealousy and backstabbing. Caitie tried to stay on the fringes, observing the dysfunction with morbid fascination, but occasionally she would find herself sucked into the drama.

A second after Caitie sat down, Reily looked at her watch and said, "Oh, darn, I have to go change. Maybe I'll see you after my set?"

"Maybe," Caitie said, looking around for Zoey, finding her by the bar, a fresh drink in her hand, flirting with a man who had to be close to, if not older than, her father's age.

She and Mel were alone at the table, and she couldn't help but wonder if it was no accident.

Down went the rest of the margarita.

"I guess I'm the last person you want to be sitting with," she said. It was meant to be a joke, to lighten the mood, but Mel just looked angry.

"Is that honestly what you think?"

Caitie had barely started and already she was screwing things up. "Mel—"

Mel moved to stand, and Caitie grabbed her arm. It felt rigid with tension. "I'm sorry! I didn't mean it like that. Don't go. *Please.*"

Mel paused, then sank dubiously back into her chair.

"I'm sorry for what I said in the salon." Caitie had to shout to be heard over the music.

"I shouldn't have put you on the spot like that," Mel shouted back.

"The last thing I want to do is hurt your feelings again."

Mel said something Caitie didn't catch.

She leaned in closer, straining to hear. *"What?"*

Exasperated, Mel leaned close and said, "Let's take a walk outside."

Caitie followed as Mel walked briskly past the bar, through the dining room, around a group of customers waiting for a table and out the door. The last traces of sunlight were melting into the horizon, and a gentle breeze cooled the air. Mel continued around the side of the building and through the lot, to a silver minivan parked in a dark corner at the back.

She used a key fob to unlock it and opened the front passenger's side door. Cait had a sudden vision of Mel pulling out a machine gun and mowing Caitie down in a spray of bullets. All she really did was toss her purse on the seat and open the glove box. From inside she extracted a pack of cigarettes and an orange lighter. She tapped one out and lit it, inhaling deeply.

Caitie thought of all the times she had lectured Mel about lung cancer and emphysema, and how Mel would swear she was going to quit. But every time she tried, she would inevitably turn to food to fight the withdrawal and pack on five or ten pounds.

"If you tell Nate you saw me light up, I'll deny it,"

Mel said, tossing the pack back in the glove box. "He hates it when I smoke."

As if Caitie wanted to put herself in the middle of their relationship. "It seems that the two of you are still really close."

"Of course we are," Mel said. "We have a son together."

"Most of the divorced couples I know, even the ones with kids, seem to hate each other. And the children always end up in the middle."

"We're not your average divorced couple, I guess. And we've worked really hard to get to this point. The key, we've found, is being totally honest with each other."

In Cait's experience, most men didn't do total honesty. Some didn't get past *occasionally* honest, while others wouldn't know the truth if it bit them in the behind.

"I met Cody at the thrift store," Cait told her.

"He told me."

"He's a miniature of Nate."

"Tell me about it," Mel said with a "mother's love" smile. One that swiftly faded. "But I don't want to talk about Nate and Cody. We need to talk about *us*. You and me."

What she and Mel had been through was a divorce of sorts, without all the legal hassle. "I'm sorry I hurt you."

"I wasn't just hurt. I was *crushed*. And heartbroken. I felt as if you had abandoned me. We were best friends since kindergarten. I loved you like a sister. Then you were just…gone. I thought I did something wrong. That you were mad at me."

Twist the knife a little deeper..."You never did anything wrong," Caitie told her. "I didn't mean for us to stop talking forever. I just needed time to get used to being away. Being on my own. Those first few months were really hard. I was lonely and homesick."

"Did it not occur to you that talking it out with your best friend might make you feel better?"

"I couldn't. It would have been too easy for you to convince me to come home."

"Who says I would have?"

"The one time I even mentioned the *possibility* that I might apply to an East Coast school, what did you do?"

Chastised, Mel shuffled her feet, kicking at a loose bit of asphalt. "I tried to talk you out of it."

"You *begged* me to stay in Colorado."

"You were my best friend. Of course I didn't want you to go away. And you're right—I probably would have tried to talk you into coming home...but..."

"After I settled in, I was going to call you. I was even going to suggest you come to New York and stay for a while. I thought it would be good for you to put some distance between you and your mom."

"But you never did."

"I heard about you and Nate. Suffice it to say, I felt very...conflicted."

The corner of Mel's mouth twitched, as if she was trying not to smile. "I'll bet."

"I left him. I moved on. I had no right to expect him not to do the same thing."

"You just never expected it to be me that he moved on with."

Cait nodded. "It felt like the worst kind of betrayal."

"Nate was a mess after you left. The poor guy was heartbroken. And, frankly, so was I. That's what drew us together."

Did she mean to imply that by leaving, Caitie had unknowingly thrust them into each other's arms? Good to know. "You fell in love?"

Mel laughed. "No, but we did get drunk and have sex. Nine months later I had Cody."

Caitie was sure Mel was only saying that to spare her feelings. "And *then* you fell in love?"

"Do I love him? Absolutely. He's one of my best friends. He's the father of my son. Am I *in love* with him? Was I ever? I sure wanted to be. I *tried* to be. I was desperate to have what you and he had. And for a short time I had myself convinced we would grow to love each other. For Cody's sake."

"But…?"

"Suffice it to say, it just wasn't meant to be."

It shouldn't have been a relief, yet it was. After so many years of believing he'd chosen Mel over her, it was difficult to reconcile reality with her childish assumptions. Now she understood why her mom was so adamant about getting them talking. "Since it happened so fast, I assumed that you and Nate probably already had feelings for each other but didn't want to hurt me, that my leaving finally left you free to date each other."

Mel's eyes widened. "Are you *crazy?* We both felt so miserable. And ashamed."

And Caitie felt ashamed now for her own wild assumptions. She could only imagine how conflicted they must have felt. Nate had always wanted a family, but knocking up his ex's best friend in a drunken one-night stand probably wasn't what he'd had in mind.

Though it was none of her business, she couldn't resist asking. "How did Nate take it when you told him you were pregnant?"

"The first words out of his mouth were *marry me*."

For some reason that made Caitie smile. She would have expected no less of him. She and Nate had had a scare once, a few months before they'd graduated. She had completely freaked, and he couldn't have been more calm and rational. She was sure that inside he was freaked out, too, and just didn't want to make her feel bad. But when the test came back negative, Nate had actually looked disappointed, and that had completely freaked her out. She wasn't ready to have a family.

Did she want kids eventually? Of course. But she needed to learn who she was before she even considered taking on the responsibility of raising a child.

"I knew Nate didn't love me," Mel said. "But I said yes. I was terrified. I had no idea how I would manage alone with a baby. My mom made it clear that I would get no help from them. All she seemed to care about was how fat I would get, and what she would tell the ladies at bingo. I let myself believe that over time we would learn to love each other, but the marriage just didn't work."

"When I left, I figured he would be upset for a couple of weeks, then realize how much better off he was without me," Caitie told her. "How much better he could do."

Mel blinked. "Why would you think that? The guy was crazy about you."

"I had myself convinced that Nate deserved better than me."

"Better?"

"I thought he deserved someone prettier and more outgoing. Someone like...well, *you*."

Mel looked puzzled. "You thought that Nate liked fat girls?"

Caitie sighed heavily. Not this tired old argument again. "I don't care what your mom used to say, you were *not* fat."

Mel rolled her eyes. "I was five feet tall and wore a size eleven. I was fat."

"You were also beautiful and fun. And *nice*. And you still are."

"So were you!"

"I didn't think so back then."

Mel ground the cigarette into the pavement with the toe of her shoe, shaking her head. "I swear you are the dumbest smart person I've ever met."

That was becoming increasingly evident. "I never knew my leaving would create such a mess."

Mel rolled her eyes. "Oh please. Don't give yourself so much credit. The decisions that Nate and I made are not your responsibility."

So why did she *feel* responsible? "If I had stayed—"

"Something different would have happened. The possibilities are endless. We can keep rehashing this over and over trying to make sense of it and drive ourselves crazy with what-ifs, or we can leave the past in the past where it should be and move on."

"Do you think we could be friends again?" Cait asked.

Tears brimmed in Mel's eyes. "I'd like to try. I've missed you."

Emotion left a knot in Cait's throat. "I missed you, too."

They threw their arms around each other and hugged, and a weight of ginormous proportions seemed to lift from Cait's shoulders. She hadn't realized until now just how much she still missed Mel.

"Are you two hugging or wrestling?"

Chapter Nine

Caitie and Mel turned to see Nate walking toward them, thumbs in his belt loops, casual as you please, gravel crunching against the soles of his cowboy boots.

"Hugging," they said in unison, then looked at each other and laughed.

"And all is right with the world," Nate said with a smile. A *real* smile, dimples and all. One that Caitie felt all the way to her knees. He stopped several feet from them, equally close to both women. And for what seemed like an awfully long time, no one said anything.

Finally Mel looked at Nate, then over to Caitie, and said in a singsong voice, *"Awkwaaaard."*

Nate shook his head. "Nope. We're just three friends hanging out at the bar."

It would be nice if that were true. If it could happen someday. Anything was possible. Though Caitie wouldn't get her hopes up.

From inside the bar she heard the jukebox cut out and the band began to warm up.

"I don't want to miss the first set," Mel said, looking from Caitie to Nate. "I'll see you guys inside?"

Would she? Maybe it would be better if Caitie left. She came here to set things right with Mel and she had done that. Would she be pushing the limits to stay? Especially with Nate's girlfriend waiting for him inside.

Cait glanced over at Nate.

"We'll be right in," he answered for the both of them.

Caitie listened to the click of Mel's heels as she walked through the lot to the front door. When she was out of earshot, Nate turned to Caitie and said, "Okay, spit it out."

She blinked. "What do you mean?"

"It was obvious you have something to say to me," he said. "I assume it has to do with whatever you and Mel talked about."

"Would you please stop doing that," she said.

"Doing what?"

"Reading my mind! It's…annoying." Especially since she hadn't the foggiest clue what he was thinking or feeling. She never had been able to get a good read on him. He let people see what he wanted them to see. Even her. Superficially, she had known practically everything about him, but she rarely knew what was going on inside his head. Or in his heart.

"It's nothing personal," he said. "I'm a cop. I read people. It's a habit."

So what he was saying was it had absolutely nothing to do with the fact that they used to date, or that he still felt some sort of connection to her.

She wasn't sure how to feel about that.

"Why didn't you tell me the circumstances around you and Mel getting married?" she said.

He shrugged. "You didn't ask."

"If I had asked, would you have told me?"

"I guess it would have depended on why you wanted to know."

"Because God forbid you might slip and say what you're really feeling." She regretted the observation, and the tone in which she had delivered it, the instant it left her mouth. She sounded like a jealous ex-girlfriend who had never gotten closure, never moved on.

Is that what she was? *Jealous?*

"Are we talking about me and Mel, or me and you?" he asked.

She honestly wasn't sure anymore.

She should have stopped right there, turned on her heel and marched back inside. Instead her lips kept right on flapping, probably making matters worse. "Please stop doing that."

"What am I doing now?"

"Don't be so vague and elusive. I hate that. Do guys think that makes them sexy and mysterious or something?"

He looked genuinely puzzled. "I didn't realize that I was being elusive."

"You *always* used to do that. I never knew what you were thinking. Half the time I felt as if I was walking around with a blindfold on."

He folded his arms over his chest. "I think you're exaggerating."

Why was she making such a big deal out of this? What difference would it make now anyway? "You're right, never mind. I really just wanted to say that I'm sorry."

"About what?"

About what? "The way I left. That I didn't try to explain."

"So explain it to me now."

"The other day you said you didn't care why."

He hesitated, his eyes pinned on hers, but it was too dark now to read his expression. "I want to know."

She opened her mouth to explain, but suddenly every excuse in her repertoire sounded immature and petty. The justifications of a girl who was too insecure and stubborn—too *lazy*—to see what was right before her eyes. Or maybe she didn't *want* to see. Nate may have been close to the vest with his feelings, but there was no reason why she couldn't have asked him. Couldn't have pressed him to be honest with her.

What was it that Mel had said? That she and Nate had worked hard on their relationship. How hard had Caitie actually worked?

Mel was right. Nate had told her that he loved her, showed her in a million little ways. Any doubts she had of his feelings for her, or of her own worthiness, were her problem, not his. Young or not, if she'd had concerns about their relationship, she should have talked to him about it.

"I was young and stupid and selfish," she told Nate, and *that* was the honest truth.

"Well, you can stop beating yourself up over it," he said. "Deep down I knew something was wrong. Instead of confronting you about it, I convinced myself that I was imagining it. That we were fine. It's my own fault for not asking."

"I loved you, Nate. Leaving you was the hardest thing I've ever had to do. But I *had* to do it."

"I know that now."

Now that she had gotten started, the words and the emotions poured out of her. "I would have told you, but I was so afraid that you would try to talk me out of it."

"That's exactly what I would have done. I didn't want to lose you. I thought that if I gave you time it would pass and everything would be fine. We would get back on track. I should have tried harder."

"Maybe I was unconsciously testing you. To see if you really loved me. Maybe I left to see if you would come after me."

"I almost did."

She blinked. "You did? When?"

"You had been gone a little over a month when I came to pretty much the same conclusion you did. I was young and stupid and selfish. I wanted to be with you, even if that meant rearranging my plans."

"But…you had your entire life already mapped out. You knew exactly what you wanted."

"If I couldn't have those things with you—" he reached up, touched her cheek "—they didn't seem worth having any longer."

"You loved me so much that you would have left Paradise to be with me?"

"I was going to tell you what happened with Mel, and beg you to forgive me."

He'd loved her that much and she had just… walked away?

Suddenly she was having trouble breathing. "What did your parents say about you leaving?"

"I didn't tell anyone. I was just going to go. I had a bag packed, a flight scheduled and a hotel booked. It would have all been very romantic if Mel hadn't come by to see me the morning of my flight."

"She told you she was pregnant."

He nodded. "I was so focused on getting back to you, it took a minute to sink in that it was actually my baby."

"And you asked her to marry you."

"I unpacked my bags, and I stayed. I loved you. I wanted *you*. But I also knew that as much as I needed you to need me, you didn't. Mel did though."

She had needed him, more than he would ever know. Probably too much, which was one of the reasons she'd had to go. Why leaving had been such torture for her. But if she had known that he really loved her, that he was willing to make the sacrifices…

"Did Mel know you were coming after me?" Cait asked him. She couldn't imagine anything more tragic, more heartbreaking, than to be stuck in a relationship with a man who was in love with someone else.

"She saw my bag sitting there by the front door and asked me if I was going somewhere. I made up some story about it being full of stuff we were donating to the Salvation Army. She didn't question it. If she knew the truth, she would have been devastated."

And thank God she had been spared that pain. "It's a little ironic," Cait said.

"What is?"

"That you were planning to come to me."

"Why is that?"

"I was going to come home," she said. "I was so homesick and unhappy, I began to feel as if I'd made a huge mistake leaving. I talked to my mom about coming back home and going to school in Denver. That's when she told me about you and Mel being engaged. I assumed that you two were in love and starting a family, and that you had forgotten all about me."

There was pain in his voice. "That wasn't it at all."

"If we had just talked to each other...maybe—"

"Don't even go there," Nate said. "Don't play the what-if game. Maybe it would have worked. Maybe it wouldn't have. Point is, we'll never know."

What difference did it make now anyway? "I guess we blew our chance."

"Big-time," he said.

"Even if we were still attracted to each other...and I'm not saying I am, but if we were, we have completely separate lives now. I made a life for myself in New York. And you have a family here. Unless either of us were willing to relocate—"

"So, are you saying that you're *not* attracted to me?"

Men and their pride. "I never said that."

"And you call me elusive," he said.

He was using her own words against her. And he seemed...closer than he'd been a minute before. "I was speaking hypothetically," she told him.

"So, are you or aren't you?"

Yes, he was definitely closer now. So close she could make out his individual features in the dark. So close she had to tilt her chin up to meet his gaze. And when she did, when their eyes locked, something in the air shifted, or maybe that was just the echo of her heart pounding through her chest.

"What difference does it make?" She looked back over her shoulder toward the bar. "Won't your girlfriend be missing you?"

"What girlfriend?" he asked, but his eyes were on her mouth.

"The blonde chick."

He reached up and touched her lower lip with the pad of his thumb, sliding it from one side to the other. That used to be all it would take. A look, a caress and she would be putty in his hands. She was a virgin when they started dating. Pure as the driven snow, with every intention of staying that way until the day she said "I do," but Nate had melted her in two weeks flat.

It wasn't taking nearly as long this time.

"There were many *blonde chicks* in the bar," he said, threading his fingers through her hair. "To which were you referring?"

"The one you were dancing with."

She saw a flash of white as he grinned. "So you assumed I'm dating her?"

"A man doesn't pick up feminine products for a woman if they aren't...involved."

"The tampons were for Mel. And you can relax. The woman I was dancing with is married."

Her eyes went wide. "You're messing around with a *married woman.* Are you forgetting where you live?"

Nate laughed. "I'm not messing around with her. Her husband was deployed six months ago. He's a good friend of mine, so I keep an eye on her and their daughter. Everyone in town knows that."

"So...you *don't* have a girlfriend?"

He shook his head, traced a deliciously light trail down the column of her neck with the tips of his fingers, all the way to her collarbone. "How about you? You have anyone special in New York?"

She shook her head, and a smile curled his lips.

"So there's no reason why I shouldn't kiss you."

She thought of several, but by then it was too late. His arms were already around her, his lips pressed to hers.

She moaned, or maybe it was him, or it could have been both of them. After all this time he still smelled the same, still felt the same.

Now *this* was home.

The ramifications of that thought hit her so swiftly she actually gasped. Nate took that as a cue to kiss her deeper, to tangle his fingers through her hair as he tilted her head. The side of the van came rushing at her back and he pinned her against it with the weight of his body, his thigh pressed intimately between her legs.

Caitie moaned and pressed back, and Nate mumbled an oath against her lips. She grabbed two fists full of his hair, pulling him closer, so afraid that he would stop and just as terrified of what might happen if he didn't. She could feel the ridge of his erection as he leaned into her, the heat of his body through his clothes.

He reached under her skirt and palmed her behind, lifted her leg up to wrap it around his waist, grinding against her.

Everything was happening too fast, but not fast enough. She was reaching for the zipper on his Levi's when the van let out a squawk and the lights flashed on.

She had never seen Nate move so quickly in his life.

He stepped away from her, finger-combing his hair back into place while she smoothed her skirt down.

"Is the coast clear?" she heard Mel call out.

Caitie winced. Caught in the act. "It's clear."

Nate shook his head. "Jesus, Mel, you nearly gave me a heart attack."

"I called your name—you didn't hear me. I didn't know what else to do. In my haste I left my purse in the car. I need my cell phone. And my money."

Caitie couldn't tell if she was angry or hurt or just surprised. Or maybe a combination of the three. It was an unusual situation. As Mel had said…*awkwaaaard*.

"Melanie—" she started, but Mel held up a hand to stop her.

"Caitie, it's okay." She paused. "Well, maybe not *okay*. But I'm not naive enough to think that this wouldn't eventually happen. It's a little weird, but I'll cope."

Caitie didn't want her to have to cope. She wanted Mel to be happy, to accept Caitie and Nathan's relationship as effortlessly as she had in high school. She wanted the past seven years to melt away, so she and Mel could go back to the way things used to be.

Nate opened the van door, grabbed Mel's purse and handed it over. "We'll be back inside in a minute."

Melanie nodded, then walked away, without the usual spring in her step, and it broke Cait's heart.

"I feel horrible," she said, collapsing against the van.

Nate stuffed his hands in his pockets, as if to signify that they were in fact very finished. "I guess we didn't think this one through."

Story of her life. "That doesn't mean we can't be friends. If you want to be, that is."

"I'd like that," he said.

"Maybe you and Mel and Cody could come visit me in New York."

"Cody would love that. Since they learned about the Statue of Liberty in preschool he's been nagging us to take him."

This could work, she realized, genuine hope lifting her heart. They could be friends. The trick was going to be remembering that Mel, Nate and Cody were a family unit, one that she would never be a part of. Taking care of them was always going to be Nate's number one priority. As it should be. It was critical that she never lost sight of that, that she respected his and Mel's relationship. If her feelings for Nate were to cause a rift between him and Mel, she would never forgive herself.

Hadn't she caused enough damage already?

Neither he nor Mel seemed to hold her responsible for the series of events that brought them to this place, but there was no escaping the facts. If not for her leaving, none of this would have happened. They had worked hard on their relationship, and she had no right to come along out of the blue and mess with that.

As far as she was concerned, she and Nate could never be anything but friends.

Chapter Ten

Monday morning Caitie dragged herself out of bed early and got to work on the landscaping. She had meant to have it all finished by now, or at least mostly done, but she'd spent all weekend cooped up in her dad's office at the diner bringing the restaurant's financial information up-to-date.

She loved her dad to death, and she knew he meant well, but a few more months at the rate they were going and he might very well have run the business into the ground. There was no doubt that Caitie had inherited her head for business from her mom.

Her dad hadn't fared much better with ordering the supplies. On some items they were ridiculously overstocked, others they barely had enough to get by until the next order went out. Making matters worse, their distributor had been bought out by a bigger company several months back, one that typically catered to large chain restaurants. While some of the bulk items were a little cheaper, prices on other things skyrocketed. They needed to look for a new, more reasonable distributor willing to work with small, mom-and-pop-type establishments.

Before starting in the garden, Caitie checked in with her headhunter. When he told her no one was responding to the résumés he'd sent out, she was almost relieved. For now at least, she had plenty to do to keep her busy here. In fact, now would be a very inconvenient time to have to fly to another city for a job interview. Her current salary was nonexistent at this point, but then so were her expenses, and the satisfaction of helping her parents was motivation enough to stick around for a while.

Around eleven her mom stepped out onto the porch to survey her progress. "What are those shrubs under the kitchen window? With the variegated leaves."

"Boxwoods."

"They're so pretty. You seem to have a natural eye for this."

Cait forced a smile, while on the inside her heart was breaking. She'd planted those shrubs Friday, and this was the third time since then that her mom had commented on them and praised Caitie's natural eye. Her long-term memory for the most part appeared sound, but her short-term memory was like Swiss cheese. Holes everywhere. If her dad hadn't told Caitie the truth, she would have figured out herself in another day or two how bad things really were.

"I wish I could help you," Betty said, looking wistfully to the naked flower bed along the side of the porch. "I used to love working in the garden. Maybe if I wore a hat and dark sunglasses…"

"Is it worth risking a headache?"

She sighed, looking regretful. "I suppose not."

Not to mention that it was far too hot for her mom to be sitting in the sun anyway. A heat wave had rolled through Saturday and settled in for an extended stay. A few degrees hotter and Caitie would have to pack it in for the day.

"Did you call Marilyn?" she asked her mom.

Looking puzzled, she said, "Marilyn who?"

"From the middle school band boosters. I left a note on the kitchen table for you. She wants you to call her back."

"She's probably recruiting volunteers. I'm just not feeling up to it."

"I didn't expect you to volunteer, but you should at least give her a call and let her know that you aren't available."

"Or she'll figure that out for herself when I don't return her call."

Caitie wasn't sure if it was pride or vanity, or maybe even embarrassment, but her mom still hadn't told anyone about her condition, and in the process of hiding her symptoms she had almost completely isolated herself from everyone in town. Even her closest friends. She hardly ever left the house.

"How long are you going to do this?" Caitie asked her.

"Do what?"

"Hide."

"I'm not hiding," she insisted. At Caitie's look of

disbelief, she added, "I'm *regrouping*. There's a difference. I'll start telling people when the time is right."

"And when will that be?" After all her friends finally stopped making an effort? When the disease was so advanced she could no longer remember anyone's name? What a lonely and sad way to live.

"I just hate seeing you so isolated."

"When the time is right, I'll just know it," Betty said, and she sounded so confident, so sure of herself, Caitie almost believed her. Almost. What if the right time had come and gone and she'd forgotten it?

Caitie wasn't about to let this drop. If her mom didn't crawl out of her cave soon, Caitie would have to take matters into her own hands.

"My goodness," her mom said, fanning her face. "It's hot as blazes out here."

"You should feel it in the sun," Caitie said, swabbing the sweat off her forehead with the hem of her tank top. In a couple of hours this side of the house would be in shade. She knew she should probably wait until then to continue. It wasn't worth getting heatstroke.

Caitie heard a car engine and turned, surprised to see Mel's van pulling up the driveway. After they'd gotten over the awkwardness of the parking lot incident, with the help of a pitcher of margaritas and several tequila shots, she and Mel had had a blast Friday night. And they already had plans to do it again this Friday.

Caitie turned to her mom, just in time to catch her darting back into the house. *Not hiding, huh?*

Mel stopped close to the house, rolled down her

window, leaned out and called, "A little hot for that, isn't it?"

Caitie walked over to the van. "I was just thinking I might have to take a break until later."

"Perfect!" Mel said. "Change into your bathing suit and grab a towel. We're going to the lake."

Fin Lake was a ten-minute drive east of town, and it was so small it was barely visible on a map and too far from any major cities to attract out-of-town visitors. To the residents of Paradise and the surrounding communities, it was their personal oasis. As teens, she and Mel and their friends had spent all their free days there, swimming, boating or just hanging out on the beach. But the real fun happened at night. Around dusk the families with young children would pack up and leave and the lake became the teenage party hot spot. They built bonfires on the beach, took midnight swims in the cool, still waters and someone always managed to sneak in a case or two of beer. Couples would often sneak off into the dense woods surrounding the area to make out and fool around. In fact, Caitie and Nate had made love for the first time on a blanket in those very woods.

Caitie wondered if after all these years she could recall the exact spot.

Only on a very rare occasion did the partying get so out of hand the police intervened. Everyone knew that if they behaved and didn't cause any trouble, local law enforcement would usually let them be.

Caitie noticed the empty booster seat in the backseat. "Just the two of us?"

"Nate and Cody, too. We both have the day off and

we promised Cody we would spend it together. They went on ahead to get a good spot close to the water."

Caitie hesitated. What Mel described sounded like a family outing, and since she wasn't a part of their family…

"I think I may just hang around here," Caitie said.

"Come on, Caitie—it'll be fun. Like old times."

"I shouldn't."

Mel frowned. "You think it's going to be awkward."

"Don't you? This is your family time."

"And as far as I'm concerned, you and I are family. So go get your bathing suit and towel and get in the van."

Caitie opened her mouth to object, but Mel cut her off.

"I'm not taking no for an answer."

Caitie recognized a losing battle when she saw one. And she couldn't deny that it sounded like fun. And terrifying. But now that she and Nate had set parameters regarding their friendship, maybe it wouldn't be *too* uncomfortable.

"Do I need anything else?" she asked Mel.

"I have a cooler stuffed with snacks and drinks and at least five bottles of sunblock with various SPF levels. All that's missing is your butt in the passenger seat."

Caitie knew that she was risking an entire day of feeling like the third, or in this case *fourth,* wheel. But she did really want to go.

Oh, what the heck. If nothing else, it would give her a chance to work on her tan. "Give me two minutes to change."

* * *

Nate sat at the very edge of the shore, the cool water lapping over his toes, watching Cody play in the sand. The hot afternoon sun baked his back and shoulders, but there was a hint of a breeze rolling across the water.

He closed his eyes and tilted his face up toward the sun, listening to the sound of children shrieking and giggling as they splashed in the water and breathing in the scent of burning charcoal and sunblock. Nate valued these days off with his family more than any other. When he was a kid his parents never had time for trips to the lake. His grandparents would sometimes take him, or he would tag along with a friend's family. When he was old enough, he and his friends would ride their bikes.

If his parents weren't at work, they were busy remodeling whichever house they lived in at the time. Flipping houses had been their preferred pastime for as long as he could remember. And it might not have been so bad if they didn't have to live in the places they were remodeling.

From the time he was in kindergarten, he left for school never knowing for sure what he would come home to. There were times when they had no kitchen, no working bathrooms. Sometimes they didn't even have running water, and he would have to bathe at his grandparents' house or use a portable toilet. Aside from holiday gatherings, he could count on one hand how many times they actually sat down and ate dinner as a family, or how many of his games they made it to in the five years he played football. It was their passion, and it took up nearly every minute of their free time.

He could recall being twelve and not coming home one night until after eleven. More than an hour past curfew. He walked into the house, which at that time was a small two-bedroom bungalow—a starter home his dad had called it—bracing himself for a lecture, or to be grounded, only to find that they had already gone to bed. He could have stayed out all night and they probably never would have noticed.

When he turned sixteen and got his first job, they began charging him rent. Reducing him, in his own humble opinion, to the status of boarder. That was part of the reason he'd loved being with Caitie's family. She used to complain about her parents giving Kelly all the attention, but he was in competition with inanimate objects, like drywall board and ceramic tile. When he was with the Cavanaughs, he felt like he was a part of the family. Even more than he did with his own parents. The Cavanaughs worked just as hard as his parents did, yet they still managed to make time for their girls, made sure they knew they were loved. Until he met them, the only families he knew of who said "I love you" were on television sitcoms or in sappy family movies.

And the first time in his life that he'd ever said the words *I love you* was to Caitie.

He had sworn a long time ago that when he had children it would be different. His kids would always come first. He would be there when they needed him. He would attend their games and activities, show up for school open houses and parent–teacher conferences. He would put aside a portion of each and every paycheck so his kids would never know the burden of student loans. His kids, barring unforeseen circumstances out of his control, would always have working plumbing, a hot meal on the table at dinnertime—even if it was just tomato soup and grilled cheese—and a solid roof over their heads.

And there were some things his kids would never do. They would never come home from school to find that all their belongings had been tossed into boxes and moved temporarily to the basement, bed included, while they put in new flooring. They would never come home after a week away at football camp to an empty house. *Empty,* meaning they forgot to tell him they made plans to move to their newest flip while he was gone.

His kids would know they ranked higher, meant more to him, than a wedge of polished granite countertop or a ceramic bathroom sink. And though the family dynamic among him, Mel and Cody wasn't his ideal, they made it work. And as his parents had gotten older, they'd taken more of an interest in his life. He and his dad had their breakfast dates, and sometimes they went to the shooting range. They had Cody over to spend the night at least once a month, and his mom babysat evenings when he and Mel were both working. It didn't make up for the past, but he'd come to realize that they had done the best they could, and even if they didn't say it, and didn't often show it, they loved him.

Nate glanced over at the blanket several yards away, where Mel and Caitie lay sunning themselves. Mel in her tummy-control one-piece, Cait in a hot-pink bikini Nate had seen her wear in high school—one he could recall taking off her on more than a few occasions. He never quite understood the allure of slathering oneself in oil and roasting under the hot sun. Mel had even gone so far as to set a timer on her phone so every fifteen minutes they could roll over and bake the opposite side. Sort of like the rotisserie chickens at the market. And in Caitie's case, just as delicious. But he wasn't supposed to be thinking like that, because according to her, they could only be friends.

The water rushed up over Nathan's feet, touching the outer wall of the sand castle Cody had been meticulously building. Like most little boys, he didn't enjoy the actual building of the structure as much as he did watching it dissolve back into the sand.

"Cody!" someone shouted.

Nate turned to the source and saw Joe Miller's little girl, Lily Ann, jumping excitedly, her blond ringlets bouncing, waving Cody over to their blanket, where her stepmom to be, Reily, and Joe's aunt Sue sat. Reily smiled and waved at Joe.

"Dad, can I play with Lily Ann?" Cody asked.

"Go ahead."

Abandoning his masterpiece without a second glance, Cody darted down the beach to join them. Nate was considering a dip in the water to cool off when someone said, "Poke me with a fork—I'm done."

He looked up to see Caitie walking toward him, her skin flushed from the sun. When Mel had announced that she was inviting Caitie to come along today, he'd had mixed feelings. Since Friday he'd been trying not to think about that kiss he and Caitie had shared. Yet he couldn't help but wonder, if Mel hadn't interrupted them, would it have ended there? Or back at his place?

And now that he'd gotten a taste of her, put his hands on her, he was just supposed to pretend that it hadn't happened?

Fat chance.

Caitie sat beside him in the sand, dipping her toes in the water, so close their thighs were nearly touching. He glanced over at Mel, who was lying on her stomach facing away from the water, oblivious to their close proximity. He knew Caitie was worried about Mel's feelings, and so was he. To a point. But if seeing him and Caitie together was a problem for her, why invite her along today?

"I forgot how much I love this place," Caitie said, digging a trench in the sand with her toes and watching it fill with water as the tide rushed in. "Do the kids still take this place over at night?"

"Yup." He glanced down at her thigh, wondered what she would do if he laid his hand there. Maybe letting Cody play with Lily Ann was a bad idea. With Cody nearby Nate had no choice but to behave. But between the youngest of the kids splashing and playing at the shore and the older kids horsing around, and the adults doing their own thing, no one was paying attention to him and Caitie.

He eyed her in his peripheral vision. Her legs were long and lean, and he could still remember the way they felt wrapped around his waist, hooked over his shoulders…

"Would you like me to leave?" Caitie asked.

"Leave?" he asked, unsure of what she meant.

"The lake. The city. The *state*. Or how about the planet?"

"Why would I want that?"

"My presence here is clearly making you uncomfortable. This is the third time I've tried to start a conversation and all I've gotten are one-word answers.

You're just sitting there eyeing me, like you're afraid I'm going to steal your watch."

He hadn't meant to be so obvious. "I'm not wearing a watch," he told her, but the quip went right over her head.

She rolled her eyes. "You know what I mean."

He lowered his voice. "I'm sitting here next to a sexy, scantily clad woman, so, yeah, I'm looking. I'm a guy. That's what we do."

"It's a beach," she said. "There are scantily clad women all over the place."

"Yeah, but I don't want to sleep with any of them."

She went very quiet and still. He glanced over at her, watched the muscles in her throat contract as she swallowed, could see her working that through, trying to gauge if he was serious or just teasing her.

Finally, she leaned in close to him, so close their bare shoulders were pressed together, and said in a low and breathy voice, "Do you remember our first time?"

She had drawn her proverbial line in the sand, and now she had just stepped over it. Meaning all bets were off.

"Not only do I remember it," he said. "I could take you to the exact spot."

Chapter Eleven

Caitie wished he would. Wished he *could*.

It wasn't often that she snubbed the rules or behaved irresponsibly, especially when that meant someone's feelings might be hurt. But there were times when being bad felt awfully good. And right now, she would do anything to go back and do it all over again, to relive that night. And she wouldn't change a single thing.

"I was so nervous, I was trembling," she told him, throwing gas on the flames. "But then you kissed me and started touching me, and I wanted you so much I forgot all about being nervous."

"There's something I should probably tell you about that night," he said, and something in his tone, in the deep furrow of his brow, sent up a big old red flag.

Her heart skipped a beat, then picked up double time. "What?"

"You know how I told you there were two other girls before you?"

Dread pooled in her belly. "Yeah."

"Well, I lied."

He *lied?* About something that important? How could he?

She was pretty sure she wouldn't want to know the real number, but she couldn't stop herself from asking. "So, how many others were there?"

From under his frown, a grin emerged. "There were no others."

She blinked, certain she'd misunderstood him. "Are you saying it was your first time, too?"

"Yup."

He had to be joking. "Why would you lie about something like that?"

He lifted one shoulder in a halfhearted shrug. "Pride. Arrogance. Stupidity. Pick one."

"You're not kidding? You really were a virgin?"

"I really was."

"But you were seventeen."

"So were you."

"Yes, but…you seemed so…*experienced.*"

He leaned closer and whispered, "I watched a lot of internet porn."

She laughed and elbowed him playfully. "You did not."

He grinned. "Well, maybe not a lot."

"I thought we were so mature, so worldly, but we didn't know anything, did we? We were just two stupid kids."

"Caitie, everyone starts out as a stupid kid."

"I think I was stupider than most. I was pathologically insecure."

"Most teenage girls are."

"No, I'm talking super insecure. From the time we started dating, I woke up every morning thinking that it would be the day you broke up with me."

"And I woke up every day thinking that you loved me as much as I loved you."

Oh man, talk about an arrow through the heart. She could actually feel it go in, felt it rip through muscle and lodge deep in her chest. "I thought you were too good for me."

"Yet here I am seven years later. Still chasing you."

She sucked in a quiet breath. "Is that what you're doing?"

"If you won't come willingly, what other choice do I have?"

If only he knew how much she wanted him. How difficult this was for her, too. "I don't want to hurt you again, Nate."

"What makes you think I would let you?"

"I'm not staying in Paradise. I have a life in New York. That's where I belong."

"And you think that would be a problem for me? Has it occurred to you that maybe all I want is sex?"

Caitie blinked. No, it had not, but it was an intriguing thought. Family man that he was, she had assumed that if they got involved, he would be expecting it to lead somewhere. That he would fall in love with her, and she would have to break his heart all over again. But if he was only interested in sex...

They heard Mel's phone alarm go off behind them and instinctively shifted apart. Mel pushed herself up off the blanket and spotted the two of them sitting at the water's edge. Caitie thought she might be disturbed seeing them together, sitting so close. But she smiled and, walking over to them said, "Who wants to go for a swim?"

Good timing since both she and Nate seemed to need a little cooling off. "Sounds like fun," Caitie said, letting Mel take her hand and pull her to her feet.

For a long time Nate sat there watching them goof off in the water. Then Cody and his friend—an adorable little girl with long blond ringlets and an impish smile—joined them, and finally Nate waded in, too. When everyone was exhausted from the water play and starving for lunch, they gathered on the blanket and dived into the sandwiches and munchies Mel had packed.

After lunch, they waited the obligatory twenty minutes, then Nate and Cody wandered off for a walk in the woods and Mel, social butterfly that she was, went to join a group of people recruiting players for a volleyball game, dragging Caitie down the beach with her. Caitie hadn't played since high school, but she held her own. When they were too exhausted to deliver another ball across the net, they let others take their place and limped away.

"I feel so old," Mel moaned as they collapsed side by side on the blanket. "Everything aches."

But it was a good ache. Caitie had almost forgotten what fun it could be to just hang around with friends, kicking back and acting goofy. It had her yearning for the past.

What if Mel hadn't gotten pregnant, and Nate had come to New York? What would Caitie's reaction have been? And where would they be today? Paradise? New York? Some other city? Would they be married? Would they be focused on careers, or would they have started a family?

What if. She could drive herself crazy overanalyzing this. In fact, she saw no point in analyzing it, period.

"This has been a really fun day," Mel said, smiling and tilting her face up to the sun. "I'm so glad you came with us."

"Me, too."

Mel opened the cooler and pulled out two beers, offering one to Caitie. "Have you made a decision yet?"

"About what?" She twisted the cap off and took a long pull from the bottle.

"Are you going to sleep with Nate?"

Caitie nearly choked on her beer. "Mel!"

"Don't even pretend that you don't want to. I saw you two whispering, and sitting close. The sexual tension was off the charts."

There didn't seem to be any point in denying it. "Wanting to and actually doing it are two very different things. And I have to say that I feel a little weird talking to you about it."

She leaned back on her elbows, casual as you please. "Why?"

Why? Was she kidding? "I would think that's obvious."

"I told you, Nate and I are friends. And as his friend I want to see him happy."

"You didn't look so happy the other night in the parking lot."

"Was I worried when I heard you were back? Yeah,

I was. I thought you were going to steal him from me. Which made me stop and realize he was never mine to steal."

Guilt jabbed Caitie good and hard. "Mel, that's not true."

"It is true. He's yours. He always has been. I was just...borrowing him. But I've been emotionally dependent on him for too long. I need to let him get on with his life, whether it's with you or someone else. And I need to get on with mine."

Caitie could feel her heart breaking for Mel. "You'll find someone."

"Why is it so easy for some people? They meet, they fall in love and they just...*know*."

"How many people have you dated since the divorce?"

Mel sighed. "Not many."

"How many is that?"

"None, actually."

She hadn't been on a date in over *four* years? Caitie lowered her voice to a whisper and said, "What about sex?"

Mel looked at her blankly. "What?"

Thinking Mel hadn't heard her, she raised her voice. "I said, what about sex?"

Looking puzzled, she said, "*Sex?* What is that?"

Caitie cringed. "I guess it's been a while."

"Six years, give or take."

Six years? That would mean that for almost two of those years she was married to Nate.

Mel knew exactly what she was thinking. "We tried for a while. I think we believed it wouldn't be a real marriage otherwise, but it just didn't feel right. Suf-

fice it to say, there was no passion. We could never get past being really good friends."

"In a weird way I feel as if I should apologize," Caitie told her. "Though I have no idea why."

"And in a weird way I feel like I should be thanking you."

Thanking *her?* "What on earth for?"

"If you hadn't left, I never would have slept with Nate, meaning we wouldn't have had Cody. Becoming a mom is the best thing that's ever happened to me. It's taught me patience and unconditional love. It's given me a whole new perspective on my own mom, and why she is the way she is. Despite being single, I'm happy with my life. More than I ever imagined I would be."

"You deserve to be happy," Caitie told her. "And you'll find someone special. I know you will. When you least expect it, you'll look up and he'll be standing there. And you'll just *know.*"

"I hope you're right."

So did Caitie.

"You never did answer my question," Mel said.

"What question?"

"If you decided to sleep with him."

"Mel—"

"All I ask is that you're discreet around Cody. At least until it gets serious."

Mel obviously had the wrong idea about this. "It's not going to get serious. I'm going back to New York."

"If you say so."

"Nate and I are not the same two people we were when I left."

"After seven years? I should hope not."

She didn't seem to be getting it. They couldn't just

pick up where they'd left off, or even start over again from scratch. He had responsibilities here. And she had…well, maybe not responsibilities, but she had friends in New York. Business contacts. And an apartment. It may have been small and ridiculously overpriced, and the furnishings secondhand, but it was hers.

Furniture can be moved, her traitorous inner voice reminded her. And there were places to rent in Paradise, really *nice* places that were a fraction of the cost. Which didn't mean much if she had no job to pay rent. Professionally there was nothing here for her.

She was going to try to explain that to Mel, but Nate chose that moment to rejoin them. He grabbed a beer from the cooler and sat down. "It must be getting close to dinnertime. I'm starved."

"Me, too. Maybe we should dive into the cooler." Mel glanced around and asked, "Where's Cody?"

Nate looked around, frowning. "Damn, I knew I forgot something."

Mel gave him a playful shove, and he laughed. "He's with a group of kids on the playground," he said.

Caitie watched the exchange with a smile. She had assumed that seeing the two of them together, teasing and joking with each other, would be awkward or even painful. But it wasn't like that at all. It made her happy to see them happy, and she would never do anything to come between them. She could never be that selfish.

All the time she had spent agonizing over Nate and Mel the past seven years suddenly seemed like a silly waste of time.

"You want me to go get him?" Nate asked.

"I'll do it." Mel hoisted herself up and slipped her feet into her sandals.

"I'll go with you," Caitie said.

"I'll just be a second! You two unpack the food." She darted off before Caitie even had time to stand up. Not only did she seem to not care if Caitie slept with Nate, but it almost seemed as if she was deliberately trying to get them alone together.

Nate opened the cooler and pulled out the containers that held their dinner: cold fried chicken, fruit salad and corn bread. Caitie's stomach rumbled so loud he heard it.

"Hungry?" he asked, wearing one of those adorable, slightly lopsided, dimpled grins that melted her brain.

Now this was the Nate that she remembered, the one she fell head over heels in love with.

"I must have worked up an appetite playing volleyball," she told him, and she realized that for the first time since losing her job, she had a real appetite. She felt hopeful, despite the fact that she had no promising job prospects on the horizon. She felt...happy. And she was pretty sure it was due in part to the man sitting on the blanket beside her. She considered telling him about her conversation with Mel, but Mel and Cody were back before she had the chance.

After dinner Cody challenged Caitie to a game of checkers and she lost. Miserably. Then the four of them took another swim, and afterward Cody passed out cold on the blanket. One by one the families with smaller children began to pack up and leave and the teenagers began to arrive.

"We should probably go," Mel said. "I have to get this boy into bed."

"I thought I was supposed to have him tonight," Nate said.

"I think I'm going to take him to the salon with me and give his hair a trim tomorrow," she said as she began to pack up their belongings.

Nate looked puzzled. "Didn't you just cut his hair last week?"

"Yes, but I didn't go short enough. He's getting a little shaggy around the ears."

Nate looked suspicious, but he didn't make an issue of it. Caitie, on the other hand, knew exactly what Mel was doing. It was one thing for her to be okay with Caitie and Nate fooling around and quite another to actually set them up.

Caitie made a point of yawning and stretching and said, "Wow, I'm exhausted. The sun really takes it out of you."

"You're not kidding," Nate said, picking up his sleeping son and hoisting him over his shoulder. "This little guy is out for the count."

As they started up the slope to the parking lot, Caitie veered off and made a quick stop at the restroom. "Don't leave without me," she joked with Mel, who she could swear had a devilish gleam in her eye.

She told herself she was imagining things, but when she made it to the parking lot, the spot where Mel's van was empty.

"Are you kidding me?" she grumbled under her breath. She should have known better than to let Mel out of her sight. She should have anticipated that she might pull something like this.

She heard the rumble of an engine and turned to see a newer-looking red pickup pull up beside her. Nate was behind the wheel. He grinned, wiggled his eyebrows and said, "Hey, baby, need a lift?"

She laughed in spite of herself. "Seeing as how my ride home left without me, I guess I do."

He leaned across the front seat and pushed the passenger's side door open for her. "Hop in."

Mel was so going to hear about this, Caitie thought as she hoisted herself up in the truck and buckled her seat belt. It was ridiculously clean inside, and still had a hint of that new car smell.

"She said she wanted to get Cody home and into bed. She asked if I would drive you." Nate pulled out of the lot and onto the road back to town. "Where to?"

"Home I guess. I want to get to bed at a decent hour so I can get up early tomorrow and work outside. Before it gets too hot."

"So, if I took you to my home…?" he asked, glancing over at her.

If only he knew how tempting that was. "I think that might be a bad idea."

He shrugged. "Couldn't hurt to ask."

"I want to. I really do. I'm just not so sure that it's a good idea."

"After Mel worked so hard to set us up?"

"I wondered if you noticed that."

"You know how she is. Once she sets her mind on something, it's tough to sway her."

"Yeah. We had a talk while you and Cody went on your walk. She more or less gave me permission to sleep with you."

"More or less?" he said, giving her a sideways glance dripping with innuendo.

"Okay, more *more* than *less*. I just don't think I'm

ready to go there. I'm not saying never. I just…I'm having these feelings, and it's confusing. I've barely been back a week and things are moving so fast." Just like the last time.

She'd made it clear from their first date that she had no intention of losing her virginity outside the sanctity of marriage. After all, waiting had never been an issue before. She'd dated guys who had tried to persuade her, but she hadn't even been tempted. With Nate it was different. He made her feel things no other boy had. When Nate kissed her, and touched her, the reasoning center of her brain shorted out and simple words like *no* or *stop* vanished from her vocabulary.

Then there was that night at the lake, on the blanket in the woods. They hadn't gone there with the intention of having sex. Nathan had never pushed her or tried to talk her into anything she wasn't ready for. He let her set the pace, let her decide when to stop and when to keep going. But that night had been special. He told her that he was falling in love with her, and she had been in love with him pretty much since their first kiss—that reckless, teenage kind of love. It was exciting and scary and she just knew that it was the right time.

She would never forget his look of surprise, or that he'd asked her about twenty times if she was sure. Though she was nervous, she had never once doubted that she wanted him to be her first, and she never regretted a second of it. And since then, no other man had ever quite measured up. No one made her *feel* the way Nate did. And she was terrified that it was happening all over again.

Chapter Twelve

When Nate turned into her parents' driveway, her dad's car was gone. Caitie thought it was supposed to be his night off.

"How has your mom been?" Nate asked, stopping by the back door.

Instead of simply answering the question, she had to go and do something stupid instead. She heard herself saying, "You want to come in and say hi?"

"Sure," he said, killing the engine.

She was tempting fate, but it was too late to change her mind now.

She was surprised to find the door locked, and the house dark and quiet as she let him in.

"Anyone home?" she called, then saw the note on the kitchen table penned in her mom's handwriting. She picked it up and read it. "Went to dinner and a show, back later."

Watching movies, especially newer releases that she'd never seen before, had the potential to be an exercise in frustration for her mom. Around the halfway point she typically forgot what had happened in the first half. But the theater in Blue Hills had dollar Mondays and they always played at least one old classic.

"So, I guess that means no one is here," Nate said, and something in his voice made the hair on the back of her neck shiver to attention. Then she made the monumental mistake of turning to look at him.

Bad idea. In that instant, her mom wasn't the only one with memory problems. Caitie could feel herself developing a severe case of verbal amnesia. He started to move toward her, his eyes pinned to hers, and rather than stopping him, her mind went blank.

"You want me to leave?" he asked.

She knew the correct answer was yes. Instead she heard herself say, "Stay."

No, no, no! This was all wrong.

Or was it?

They were both single, consenting adults, damn it. Who could they possibly hurt? Other than themselves, that is. But maybe that was a risk she was willing to take.

He stepped closer, eyes locked on hers, his arms sliding around her waist, and hers automatically circled his neck, her fingers tunneling through his hair.

He mumbled something incoherent; then his lips were on hers. She didn't say no when he grasped the shirt she'd thrown on over her bathing suit and tugged it over her head. Under her bikini top, which he swiftly untied and tossed on the kitchen floor, her skin was pale, damp and gritty with sand and dirt. And when he shoved her shorts down and she kicked them off, they left a pile of sand on the kitchen floor.

"I think we brought half the beach home with us," Nate joked.

"We'll have to do something about that," she said, pulling his shirt up over his head. She'd been dying to lay her hands on his muscular chest, touch his wide shoulders and sinewy arms, since that first day at the diner when she saw the way he filled out his uniform. And he felt just as wonderful as she'd imagined he would.

"What did you have in mind?" he asked, lifting one of her hands from his chest and kissing the inside of her wrist.

"I was thinking that we could both use a shower." The idea of soaping up and rubbing all over each other made her shiver with delight.

"*That* is an *excellent* idea," he said, but instead of simply walking up the stairs like a regular person, he had to go all caveman on her instead. He picked her up, tossed her over his shoulder and carried her up.

It could have been worse. He could have dragged her upstairs by her hair. She hoped he didn't lose his footing and kill them both. Though she couldn't recall ever seeing him unsteady on his feet. "I *can* walk, you know."

"But it's so much more fun like this," he said. "And this way you don't have the option of changing your mind."

She wasn't going anywhere. But she knew without a doubt that if she had a sudden change of heart, he wouldn't hesitate to put her down. And he was right. This was more fun.

She was almost sorry when they reached the bathroom and he set her back down again. While he shut and locked the door, she turned on the shower and adjusted the temperature. Then he was behind her, easing her bikini bottoms down, leading her under the spray. Though he was the last person she imagined she would ever be showering with, she wouldn't want to be there with anyone else. They soaped each other up, kissing and touching, taking their time, until not a single inch had gone unexplored in one way or another.

She had believed that making love to Nate could never be better than it had been in high school, but boy was she wrong. They had both learned a thing or two since then, and all that time apart had heightened their desire to an unprecedented level. It was no longer about wanting him. She *needed* to be close to him. It wasn't really even about the sex, even though that was pretty freaking fantastic. When he pinned her against the shower wall, thrust himself inside of her, she wasn't just on another planet. She was in a different *galaxy*.

They played in the shower until the water ran cold and their legs were too weak to stand; then they fell into her bed. The rest of the night was a muddle of pleasure and wonder, an orgasm-induced haze. They fell asleep curled up in each other's arms.

Were they were moving too fast, getting too comfortable too soon? She didn't know. Being with him felt so natural, and she felt so happy. But was she doing the right thing?

Her life in New York seemed a million miles away, and right then it might as well have been.

* * *

Caitie gazed up at the house, shading her eyes from the morning sun. Nate had finished painting the siding over the weekend, and he had been up on a ladder painting the second-floor gutters and window trim all morning.

"I think you missed a spot," she called up.

Without missing a stroke, he called back, "No, I didn't."

"I really think you did. There's a spot to your right that looks…funky."

He peered down at her, holding out the brush. "If you think you can do a better job, come on up."

He knew damn well she was terrified of heights. She rolled her eyes with exasperation. She didn't recall him being this difficult before. "Never mind."

When she'd asked him for the name of a good painter who was reasonably cheap, he had said he knew someone, but he would have to set it up. She didn't care, so long as the person did a decent job. But it was Nate who had showed up on the scheduled day, painting equipment in the bed of his truck.

"You're a painter?" she said as he unloaded his supplies that first day.

"When necessary. I helped my dad paint the last couple of flips he had. It's not complicated."

When she asked what he wanted as payment, he just grinned and said, "Take a wild guess."

'Nuff said.

They were building up to something; she could feel it. The more time she spent with him, the more she wanted to be with him. They had been almost inseparable this past week. Maybe it had been inevitable.

Maybe they were destined to get together again. Or maybe all the sex they'd been having was clouding her judgment.

She was riding that new relationship roller coaster, letting her emotions call the shots, riding the highs and lows. The excitement, the fear, the exhilaration.

She had been back in Paradise nearly three weeks and it was beginning to feel like home again. Or maybe deep down it had never stopped being her "true" home. When she thought about leaving again, going back to New York or even to a new city, something as close to home as Denver, she felt anxious and unsettled.

This was just moving so fast. She was torn between wanting to slam on the brakes and totally throwing caution to the wind. Was a life here with Nate really what she wanted? And is that what he wanted, too? They didn't talk about the future. Ever.

Nate pulled a cloth from the back pocket of his painter's overalls and swiped the perspiration off his forehead. Since midweek the temperature had hovered around eighty-two degrees, which was normal for early September. Personally, she was ready for some cooler weather.

"You planning to stand there and supervise?" Nathan asked.

She wouldn't call it supervising exactly….

"It would be a darned shame if I accidentally dropped a pint of black paint on your head," he added.

"No need to resort to threats. I'm going."

She walked the long way around the house, admiring the flower beds that she had just finished putting the final touches on that morning, feeling exceptionally proud of herself. It had been a very long week spent mostly on her hands and knees in the dirt, but it had been worth it. She wasn't one to brag, but for a novice, she had done a pretty darn good job. Even her parents had been impressed.

The side door opened, and her mom stepped out onto the back porch. She had looked so tired the past few days. Her headaches had been especially bad and she hadn't been sleeping well. Caitie thought she should go to the doctor, but she resisted.

"I'm tired of doctors," she had said. "They'll poke and prod me, and put me through a gazillion tests, then tell me there's nothing they can do."

Sadly, she was probably right.

"Are you two going to be around for dinner?" she asked Caitie. "I have a pot of chili on the stove."

"Sounds good," she told her mom, for what was now the third time. Inside her heart was breaking, but she forced a smile.

Though her mother's memory was fading, her powers of perception were still sharp. "Did I already ask you that?" she said.

Reluctantly Caitie nodded. She would probably ask her another three times over the course of the afternoon. The occupational therapist her mom had been seeing had suggested putting up a centrally located dry-erase board, where her mom could write down thoughts or ideas or things she needed to remember. Which in theory sounded brilliant to Caitie. Unfortunately, in the time it took her mom to actually get to the board, she'd usually forgot whatever it was she wanted to write. And even when she did remember to write things down, she often forgot to reread whatever it was.

She sighed and shook her head. "I'm sorry, honey."

And every time she apologized, Caitie's heart broke all over again. "Mom, it's okay. Anything I can do to help?"

"I don't think so. Did you finish your homework?"

"About seven years ago."

Her mom blinked, looking confused; then she must have realized what she said. The past was still so clear, she would occasionally revert back, but this time she caught herself.

"Did I just ask you about homework?" she said, and Caitie nodded. Her mom laughed in spite of herself. "I think seeing you and Nate together lately is confusing me."

That made two of them. Caitie had never felt so happy and conflicted at the same time. She knew her parents were both curious as to what was going on exactly, but they hadn't asked. But considering how often she and Nate were seeing each other, and the fact that he'd spent the night a couple of times, they had to have a pretty good idea that the relationship was physical. Beyond that, even Caitie wasn't sure what was going on.

Caitie heard the crunch of tires on the driveway and turned to see Mel's minivan.

"I had better go check on the chili," her mom said, retreating back into the house to hide.

Mel parked next to Nathan's truck and got out. She was dressed casually in denim capri pants, sparkly flip-flops and a white T-shirt that showed off a deep tan. She waved to Caitie, then opened the side door and Cody hopped out. As far as he knew, his dad and Caitie were just friends, but now that she'd gotten to know him better, she had come to realize that he was an exceptionally bright kid. Because of his dyslexia, he had to work extra hard on reading and writing, but when it came to comprehension and recall, he was off the charts. And when it came to observing the world around him, he didn't miss a thing. If he didn't already suspect that she and Nate were more than friends, it probably wouldn't take him long to figure it out.

"Hi, Caitie!" Cody half ran, half skipped to where she stood and threw his arms around her waist.

She rumpled his hair, her heart melting. When she had kids, she hoped they were just like Cody. "Hey, kiddo, what's up?"

"Me and Mommy went to Lily Ann's aunt's house today and we got to see *puppies* being born!"

"You did? That's awesome."

"They came out in sacks, and the mommy had to lick them clean. It was kinda gross but cool. Mommy said that if I'm a'sponsible, we can get one."

"I said maybe," Mel reminded him as she joined them by the porch. "A puppy is a *big* responsibility for a little boy. Especially one who forgets to clean his room, or do his morning reading lessons."

His mom's warning seemed to go right over his head. "I want to tell Daddy about the puppies."

"He's on the ladder on the other side of the house," Caitie told him. "Can you do me a big favor?"

He nodded enthusiastically.

"Tell him he missed a spot."

"Okay!" He darted off in search of his dad, and Mel watched him go, wearing an amused mother's smile.

"Refresh my memory," Caitie said. "Who is Lily Ann's aunt? I don't recall Joe having a sister."

"It's her mom's sister, Emily Stevens."

"The town vet?"

"That's the one. She and Joe are still good friends. She was there for him to help with Lily Ann when Beth split."

Emily, the oldest of seven kids, was the only success story in a family plagued by alcohol and drug use. At least two of her brothers had done hard time in prison, and Beth, Joe's ex-wife, had up and left them when Lily Ann was an infant.

"Are you really going to get him a puppy?" she asked Mel.

Mel sighed, turning to her. "He's been begging me for a puppy since he was old enough to talk, but it's such a huge responsibility. I'm just not sure if I'm ready to go there."

"Could you get him something that requires less attention, like a kitten?"

"He's allergic, just like Nate."

"I didn't know Nate was allergic."

"Neither did he, until we got a kitten. With all the moving around his parents did, they never had animals. He tried taking a couple of different kinds of allergy medication, but nothing seemed to help. After one very miserable month of sniffling and sneezing, we had to give it back to the shelter." She nodded to the porch. "Was that your mom I just saw?"

"Yeah, why?"

She chewed her lip for a second or two, looking troubled, then said, "Is she upset with me?"

"Of course not."

"Are you sure? She's been getting her hair done every four weeks since I opened the salon, but she hasn't been in for almost two months. And the last time she was in, she seemed...off. I don't even know how to explain it. I just assumed that I had said or done something to hurt her feelings."

This was the kind of thing Cait had been worried about. By not admitting the truth, her mom was hurting people who cared about her.

"If I tell you what's going on, you can't tell anyone else," Caitie said. "And I mean *no one*."

Mel frowned. "You know you can trust me."

"My mom was diagnosed with early onset Alzheimer's."

Mel sucked in a quiet breath. "Oh no. Oh, Caitie, I'm so sorry."

"No one knows yet. Except her doctors and us and the sheriff's office."

Looking surprised, she said, "Nate knows?"

Caitie nodded. "Everyone on the force does. They keep an eye on her. Or they did when she would go out."

"He never said a word to me."

When Nate made a promise, he kept it. "She's not ready for people to know yet. She's basically become a recluse."

"Why?"

"She thinks that people will treat her differently."

"I'm sure that everyone would just want to help somehow. Your mom has done so much for the city. People respect her."

"I think...I think she's embarrassed."

Mel looked like she might cry. "Caitie, I am so sorry. I wish I'd known. She was a better mom to me than my own mom ever was. If I had a problem, I always knew I could come to her."

Mel had always been like a part of the family. She was over so much during summer vacation and spent so many nights at the Cavanaughs, she had practically lived with them.

"She's not going to be able to hide it much longer," Cait told her. "Her long-term memory is still sharp, but short-term? She's having major problems. She isn't even allowed to drive anymore."

"I guess that explains why I haven't seen her around."

"I had to take over all of the bookkeeping and ordering at the diner. My dad, it turns out, is pretty useless when it comes to that sort of thing."

"Tell me about it," Mel said. "My accountant took a job in Denver, and the guy I hired to replace her is less than reliable."

"If you want, while I'm here, I can do your books for you."

Mel blinked. "Really? You would do that for me?"

"Of course."

"Just like school," she said with a grin. "When you helped me with my math homework."

"I could even teach you how to do them yourself. The program I use does most of the work for me. It's not as difficult as people think."

"But it is time-consuming. That's my main problem. And in answer to your question, yes, I would love it if you could do my books. Just let me know how much you charge."

"Mel, I'm not going to charge you."

She could see Mel digging her heels in. "And I won't let you do it for free."

This was one of those losing arguments. But she had no clue what the going rate would be for a small-town bookkeeper. "Tell you what. I'll charge you what your current guy charges."

"That sounds fair," Mel said.

Her timing was good. With the landscaping all finished, and the painting almost done, Caitie needed something to keep her busy.

"So, when you said you can do it while you're here," Mel asked, "does that mean you're still planning to go back to New York?"

"If I can ever find a job there. I may have to settle for another city."

"Like where?"

"Chicago, L.A., Dallas. Wherever someone will hire me."

"Why don't you stay here?"

The thought had crossed her mind. Fleetingly.

Okay, maybe a *bit* more than fleetingly. Maybe if Nathan were to tell her he loved her and ask her to stay, she would seriously consider it, but she wasn't counting on anything at this point.

"And do what?" she asked Mel. "Paradise is short on high-profile finance firms."

"Why don't you start your own business?"

"What kind of business."

"Finance, bookkeeping. It wouldn't be high profile. Not at first anyway. But it would be yours. Heck, you already have two clients. Unless it's the money you're concerned about."

That wasn't it. The money was nice, sure. She liked

the security of having a substantial money reserve in her savings account. But the idea of working those crazy hours again? It no longer held the appeal it once had. If she ever planned to get married and have a family, the clock was ticking. Did she want to be one of those moms whose kids were raised by a nanny while she worked ridiculous hours, or did she want to be a hands-on mom? Or even a stay-at-home mom? She could keep a home office, work from there while Nate—

Whoa...she told herself to hold on right there. She didn't even know if Nate would want to marry her, much less have a baby with her. He said all that he wanted was sex, and since then he had never once indicated that he would ever want it to be more than that. In a short time they had gone from being enemies, to frenemies, to friends, to friends with benefits. Where did they draw the line?

As if she were reading Caitie's mind, Mel said, "He needs you, you know. He may not want to admit it, but he does. Since you've been back it's the happiest I've seen him in a long time. He wants you to stay. He's just too proud to say so."

And perhaps she was too proud to admit she wanted to stay, too.

Chapter Thirteen

Cody was still going on about the puppies when he and Nate came walking around the side of the house. "Mommy! Dad says maybe I can get a puppy for my birthday!"

Mel shot Nate a look. "Sweetheart, you just had a birthday last month. You won't have another one for almost a whole year."

Cody frowned. "Oh."

Mel ruffled her son's hair, which earned her a grumble from Cody. "We had better get going, kiddo. We have errands to run."

Cody pouted and said, "Aw, man. Can't I stay here with Dad?"

"Not today."

"I promise I'll be good. Pleeeeease! I won't get on the ladder. Or bug Dad at all."

Caitie considered telling them that there was still a box of old sports equipment in the garage he could play with if he really wanted to stay, but in a tone of firm authority, Nate said, "Listen to your mom."

Cody didn't argue, but he did sulk and drag his feet all the way to their van. Caitie waited on the porch step while Nate kissed and hugged them both goodbye, then came over to sit beside her. "Everything okay?"

She realized she was frowning and flashed him a smile. "Yeah. Everything is great."

Nate slipped an arm around her shoulder, and she laid her head against his chest, felt a quickening of her pulse and an ache in her heart.

"There's something you're not telling me," he said.

Oh, he had no idea. "I'm worried about my mom," she said, which wasn't completely untrue. "She needs to get out more, see people."

"I'm finished with the trim. Why don't we take your mom out to lunch."

She blinked. "Out?"

"Yes, out. At an eating establishment."

"Like…a date?"

"Like lunch. I was thinking Joe's Place."

Lunch could be a date. And even if it technically wasn't, there would be repercussions he obviously hadn't taken into account. "If people see us together like that, they'll start talking."

He shrugged. "So what?"

"It doesn't bother you at all?"

"Should it?"

If he didn't think so…

"Give me a minute to clean up the paint equipment, then we can go," he told her.

She stepped inside to look for her mom and found her in the recliner in the den, taking a nap.

"Mom…?" Caitie gave her shoulder a gentle shake, but she didn't budge.

Through the den window she heard a clatter from the side of the house; then Nate swore. Loudly.

Thinking he may have fallen off the ladder, she rushed outside and around the house, stopping short when she saw Nate standing at the foot of the ladder, black paint in his hair and dripping down the left side of his body. It was also on the ladder, the grass and splattered on the newly painted siding.

And boy did he look mad.

"What happened?"

He glared at her. "Take a guess."

She bit her lip to keep from laughing.

"It's not funny."

No, it was very funny. In the white overalls he looked like a lopsided skunk.

"You want to grab the hose for me?" Nate said. "I have to rinse off the siding before the black stains it."

"It won't take the new paint off?"

"I hope not."

"Hold on." She hurried around the other side of the house and unwound the hose. She turned the water on, giving her new flower beds a quick misting as she dragged the hose around the house. Nate was still standing by the ladder, using a rag to wipe whatever paint he could from his hair, mumbling to himself. He really was a mess. He would definitely need a shower before he went anywhere, unless…

She looked at the hose, then at Nate, and an idea began to form. A wonderfully *evil* idea.

Was it mean? Probably. Would it make him angry? Possibly.

Could she live with that?

Absolutely.

Feeling a giddy sort of excitement, she adjusted the sprayer to the jet setting, aimed, pulled the trigger and fired.

The instant a jet of icy water slammed the side of his head, Nate knew that asking Caitie to get him the hose had been a mistake. The force of the water snapped his head to one side and diluted black paint poured down his face. It burned his eyes and nose and soaked his clothing.

Caitie probably though she was being funny, but as far as he was concerned, she had just declared war.

Holding a hand up to ward off the spray, Nate charged her. She let out a shriek as he caught her around the waist and took her to the ground like a sack of flour, their landing cushioned by the wet grass. He figured that would be enough to knock the hose from her hands, but she was still holding on and still spraying, only now she was getting herself just as wet and paint smeared as he was.

They wrestled with the sprayer, and, with an astonishing amount of effort, he finally pried it from her hands and tossed it several feet away. Caitie dove for it.

"Oh no, you don't!" The woman was ruthless. He caught her just inches from the nozzle and grabbed her wrists. She fought him, but he managed to roll her onto her back, holding her to the ground with his full weight, pinning her wrists on either side of her head.

"Oh my God," she groaned, struggling against his grip. "You weight a *ton*. I can't breathe."

"Did you think I would just stand there and let you pummel me?"

"I was just trying to be helpful."

"Helpful?"

She was the picture of innocence, but she had what could only be described as a devilish spark in her eyes. "Honestly, I thought you would be thanking me."

"No, you didn't."

She grinned up at him. "No. I didn't. I just wanted to make you suffer."

With her wiggling around underneath him, he was definitely suffering. If she would slide her leg just slightly to the left…

She gave one last valiant effort to break free, then went limp. "Screw it. I give up."

He let her wrists go but kept her body pinned. Mostly because it felt good. Because being close to her made him feel…complete, almost as if a switch had been flipped. As if a part of him had just woken up after a long, deep sleep. Or maybe she had taken a part of his heart with her when she'd left, and he was just now getting it back.

Whatever the reason, he was falling in love with her. Maybe he had never stopped.

"Can you get off now?" Caitie asked.

Talk about a loaded question. He slid one thigh intimately between her two. "With your help, I'm sure I could."

She sucked in a breath as his knee grazed the crotch of her shorts. He took her hand, pressed a kiss to the inside of her wrist, her palm. She smelled like earth and sunshine, which he never would have considered erotic. Until now. Everything about her turned him on, and it was getting increasingly more difficult to shut that down. To pretend that it was just sex to him.

He kissed her shoulder, her neck, working his way up. "You taste delicious," he said.

"My mom is asleep in the den. We could sneak upstairs and take a shower together."

They were both adults, and her parents obviously knew what was going on, yet he felt it was disrespectful to fool around right under their noses. "Or we could go to my house," he said.

"And risk one of your neighbors seeing us? The news will make it all over town in ten minutes flat."

Here we go again. He stopped short of rolling his eyes. "My relationship with you is no one else's business."

"People will make it their business."

Of course they would, but that wasn't his or Cait's problem. "You worry too much about what other people think."

Looking puzzled, she said, "You honestly don't care if people know about us."

He pushed himself up and sat in the grass, looking down at her. "Caitie, I really don't."

"What about Mel?"

"What about her?"

"You're not worried that her feelings might be hurt?"

Was she kidding? "After she tried so hard to get us back together? Why would she be hurt?"

"I just thought it would be weird for her. And you, too, when I leave again."

"I think you're making this more complicated than it has to be," he said.

"What if I didn't?"

"Didn't make it complicated?"

"Didn't leave."

His heart skipped a beat, but he refused to get his hopes up. As he'd told her before, he no longer played the what-if game. "I didn't realize that was a possibility."

"I could probably be persuaded."

If she was expecting him to beg her to stay, she was in for a disappointment. His days of chasing her were over. Either she wanted him or she didn't. Either she wanted to stay or she wanted to leave. There was no gray area.

Did he want her to stay? Did he want to give their relationship another try? Absolutely. But until she made a decision about leaving or staying, the subject was closed as far as he was concerned.

"I guess we'll deal with that when the time comes," he said.

She frowned, looking frustrated. She started to say something else, but then he heard her mom call out in a slightly frantic tone, "Caitie! I need help!"

Caitie jumped up so fast she nearly knocked Nate over. He jumped up, too, and followed her around to the back door. Betty stood on the porch looking shell-shocked, staring down at the palms of her hands with what looked like chili splattered up the front of her jeans.

"Mom, what happened?" Caitie asked her, taking her hands to inspect them. They were both beet-red, and Betty looked dazed, as if she wasn't quite sure what was happening.

"I burned my hands on the pot," she said.

"Let's go inside," Caitie said, leading her into the kitchen, where the real mess was. There was a mostly empty pot on the floor by the stove and chili everywhere. It was on the floor and up the walls and running down the front of the stove. She'd even managed to get it on the kitchen table and a couple of the chairs.

Caitie guided her mom over to the sink and ran cold water over her hands. Betty winced. Nate grabbed the trash can and a roll of paper towels from under the kitchen sink and started cleaning up the mess.

"How did this happen?" Caitie asked.

Betty's voice sounded wobbly and her face looked pale, as if she might faint. "I picked the pot up, but I guess I forgot that it was still hot."

"You didn't use pot holders?"

Betty shook her head, gazing down at her blistering hands as if she wasn't really seeing them. "I guess not."

"I have to call Dad."

Betty's eyes widened, and she pulled her hands free. "No, you don't."

"Yes, I *do*."

"This was just a stupid accident. It'll only make him worry."

For good reason. "Mom, you need to go to the clinic."

"No, I'll be fine," she insisted, but when she tried to dry her hands, she let out a gasp of pain.

Caitie grabbed her hands and evaluated the damage. "Mom, you're blistering. You really need to see a doctor."

"I don't want to upset your dad."

"He's going to be even more upset when your hands get infected and fall off. I'm calling him."

She tried to argue, but Caitie wouldn't listen, and Nate didn't blame her. Betty obviously needed medical attention.

Nathan worked on cleaning up the mess while Caitie called her dad; then she took her mom upstairs to help her change into clean clothes.

Lou came charging in what seemed like only a few minutes later. Being a cop, Nate didn't even want to know how fast he must have driven to get there so quickly. He was still wearing his apron from the diner and a look of barely contained panic. Nate could swear he'd aged ten years in the past couple of months. It was obvious that the poor man was running himself ragged.

"Where's my wife?"

"She's okay. Caitie took her upstairs to change. She had chili all over her clothes."

"You don't have to do that," he said, nodding to the mess. "I can clean it up later."

"I don't mind," Nate told him.

"She's getting bad," Lou said. "I can't be here all the time. What am I going to do when she can't be left alone?"

"You'll figure something out," Nate assured him. "Everything will work out."

"I don't know what I would do without Caitie. She's been such a huge help. I'm not sure if I can do this on my own."

If Caitie decided to leave, he would have to. "You could ask her to stay."

"Or you could," Lou said.

He wished that were an option. "I can't do that."

"You love her, don't you? You want her to stay."

That just wasn't reason enough. "*She* has to want to stay. If I tried to persuade her against her will, I would only be delaying the inevitable."

As if seeing him for the first time since he'd raced in the door, Lou looked Nate up and down and said, "What the hell happened to you?"

Caitie happened to him. He couldn't think clearly when she was around. "I spilled paint and your daughter got a little hose happy."

Lou actually cracked a smile. But before he could respond, Caitie walked into the kitchen, still in her wet, stained clothes.

"Where is your mom?" Lou asked her.

"In the bathroom."

"Alone?"

"She said she'll be right down. That she isn't so bad she can't use the damned bathroom alone."

Nate could imagine Caitie in a similar situation being just as hard-nosed and stubborn.

"I don't think she should be allowed to use the stove unsupervised anymore," Caitie told her dad. "A couple of days ago she left a burner on under a dirty pan when she laid down for a nap. If I hadn't been home, she could have burned down the house."

Lou frowned. "Why didn't you tell me?"

"She begged me not to. She said it was an honest mistake. I think this latest incident proves otherwise."

Distress deepened the lines of worry in his forehead. "But…she loves to cook."

"Today it's burned palms. What will it be next time?"

Lou sighed, clearly seeing her point.

"Another incident like this and we won't be able

to leave her alone at all," Caitie told him. "It's getting too dangerous."

"I know," he said. "I just really hoped we had more time before her memory became a major issue."

"I think we're pretty much there," Cait told him. "And while I'm not crazy about the idea, we could call Kelly. I know she's not the most responsible person, but she could help. Maybe she could take a semester off."

"She dropped out," Lou said.

Caitie's jaw went slack. "Dropped out? Who told you that?"

"She did. I called her last week, to explain the situation with mom and the Alzheimer's. She told me then. Apparently she met someone and has been living with him all summer."

"Did she say *why* she quit school?"

He shook his head. "I asked her when her classes start, and she said she was taking some time off. That's all I know. Frankly, I have enough on my plate. Kelly is an adult. She has to make her own choices, then be mature enough to live with them."

Nate knew that if Caitie had talked to Kelly, she would have gotten answers from her sister. Lou didn't like to rock the boat. Right now, Nate couldn't say he blamed him. The man had too much to deal with already. He didn't need to be worrying about his wayward daughter.

Caitie's mom stepped into the kitchen, putting an end to the conversation. She looked pale and tired. "I'm ready to go," she said.

"Should I go with you?" Caitie asked.

"There's really no point," her mom said. "We'll

probably just spend a lot of time sitting around waiting."

"Let me at least help you into the car."

"I'm not an invalid," her mom snapped.

Caitie put on a good face, but Nate could feel her frustration. "I thought that with burned hands you may need help with your seat belt."

"I'll help her," Lou said.

Caitie nodded, looking like she wanted to cry. "Call me after you see the doctor."

Lou led his wife out the door, and Caitie watched them through the window. Nate stepped up behind her and wrapped his arms around her. She leaned into him, laying her head back on his chest. They stood that way until the car was out of sight; then she turned and burrowed into his arms.

"This sucks," she said, her voice muffled against his damp shirt. "How can I leave her like this? What if I come back home in a month and she doesn't remember me?"

It took everything in him not to encourage her to stay. Like he'd told Lou, it was her decision to make. And considering how upset she was, she was in no shape to be making any life-altering decisions. "Her long-term memory is still sharp. I don't think you'll have to worry about that for a long time."

"I'm scared for her."

"Me, too," he said, holding her tighter.

"I told Mel about her."

"I know. She mentioned it when we were saying goodbye. She wants to help somehow. I think that when people learn what's happening, a lot of them are going to want to help."

"Try telling my mom that. She's so damned stubborn. I suppose we could be sneaky about it. We could tell everyone, then tell her that she did it and just doesn't remember."

"Somehow I doubt that would work."

She was quiet for several minutes. When she looked up at him, her eyes were so full of conflict it made his heart hurt. "What are we doing?"

"I'm not sure what you mean."

"Us. Me and you. Is it an affair? Friends with benefits? I know we said just sex, but it's not feeling like just sex to me anymore. To be honest, it never did."

Not for him, either, but that was beside the point. "Maybe now isn't the best time to discuss this."

She took a step back, out of his arms. "If not now, then when? I need to figure out what I'm doing...what I'm going to do."

"When you figure it out, we'll talk."

"But how can I figure it out if we don't talk?"

"Because what I think doesn't matter. This is one decision you'll have to make on your own."

"But—"

"You're not going to win this one."

"Will you at least tell me why?"

He just stared at her.

"Should I take that as a no?"

She could bully him all she wanted. He wasn't going to change his mind. She was looking for a reason to stay, an excuse to justify it, but she wasn't going to get it from him. If she was going to move back to Paradise, it would have to be because *she* wanted to.

Chapter Fourteen

Caitie called her sister twice a day for the next five days. She left messages, all but begged Kelly to call her back. A week passed, then another, and Caitie had to resign herself to what she had always suspected. Kelly genuinely didn't give a damn.

Caitie did, however, receive a somewhat cryptic call from Joe Miller. He asked if she could stop by the bar the next day, but he didn't say why. She couldn't imagine what it could be about, but she agreed to meet him. They picked a time after the lunch rush, and when she got there, instead of chatting over a drink at the bar, Joe led her back to his office and offered her a seat. And Joe being Joe, there was no small talk or beating around the bush. He got right to the point.

"We had our chamber of commerce meeting last

night," he told her. "Melanie Jefferies was telling us that you've started doing the books for her salon."

"I'm doing the books at the diner, too," she said, unsure of why Joe would care either way.

"Well, I wanted to catch you before you're all booked up."

Confused, she said, "All booked up with what?"

"Clients. At least a dozen people asked her for your number."

And she *gave* it to them? "Are you saying that you want to hire me to do your books?"

"Well…yeah. That's exactly what I'm saying."

"And there are others?"

"At least a dozen. And when word gets around, probably more."

She was almost too stunned to reply. "I don't know what to say."

"How about, 'Sure, Joe. I'd love to do your books.'"

She smiled. "Of course I would. But the thing is, I'm not sure how long I'll be here."

"Melanie gave the impression that you were here to stay."

Oh did she? Mel knew damn well that Caitie hadn't yet made a decision. Caitie wanted to stay. At least, she was pretty sure she did. It had been so long since she'd heard from her headhunter that she was positive he'd given up on her. And her parents definitely needed her help. The only thing holding her back was Nate. He still refused to talk about the future with her. And he refused to tell her why. She felt a little as if she were flying blind.

"Can you give me a week to think about it?"

"Sure. Take all the time you need. The bar isn't going anywhere."

It was looking more and more like she wasn't, either. Even if she could find another job in New York or some other major city, she could hardly imagine herself taking it. But this was a life-changing decision and one she would be locked into for a very long time. Probably the rest of her life. She wanted to be sure that she was doing the right thing this time. This was her last chance to get it right.

She left her car parked in the street by Joe's and walked to the salon. One of the stylists was sitting on the bench out front, smoking a cigarette and texting on her phone.

"Is Mel here?" Caitie asked her.

"She's in her office," the girl told her, not even looking up from her phone. Caitie's presence in town was far from the spectacle it had been a month ago, and she was relieved. She hated nothing more than being the center of attention. Which is why she insisted that she and Nate keep the true nature of their relationship under wraps. At least until their future was a bit clearer.

Caitie let herself into the salon, waving hello to everyone as she walked to Mel's office in back. She was on the phone when Caitie knocked, but Mel smiled and waved her inside, pointing to the seat opposite her desk.

After several minutes of arguing about a botched hair color order, she hung up and turned to Caitie. "I didn't expect to see you today. What's up?"

"I had an interesting meeting with Joe Miller."

"What did he want?" she said, the picture of innocence, but Caitie wasn't buying it.

"Apparently *someone* at the chamber of commerce meeting was giving people my number. He wants to hire me to do his books. I don't suppose you know anything about that."

"Me?"

Caitie glared at her, and Mel knew she was busted.

"It's not what you're thinking," Mel said.

"What did you tell him?"

"All I did was mention that I fired the clown who was doing my books. When they asked me who I was using now, I said you. But it's not as if I was out trying to drum up business for you."

"Well, according to Joe, I should be expecting quite a few calls."

"Look at your résumé. Who wouldn't be impressed? And at least now you know that you have options if you do stay. You could have a lucrative business, and you would be working for yourself, which I can say from experience is very cool. You could make your own hours, so you have time to help your mom and dad."

Caitie couldn't deny that sounded appealing. She'd never considered the possibility of starting her own business. She could work out of her parents' house for now. The start-up cost would probably be minimal. As her clientele grew, she could look into renting office space. Or she could rent a house and have a home office. Or maybe at some point Nate would ask her to move in with him. In that case they would need a bigger place. Currently he was renting from his parents. A tiny, remodeled two-bedroom ranch that had no space for a home office. Or a baby, if she and Nate decided to start a family.

Her pulse quickened when she imagined them building a life together. And the more she thought about it, the more excited she began to feel. If she could stay in Paradise with Nate and still salvage her career, it would be like a dream come true. Which of course made her wonder, *What's the catch?*

Or maybe there was no catch. Maybe this was the "opportunity" she'd been waiting for.

"You're seriously considering it, aren't you?" Mel said, looking hopeful.

"I think I am."

"Nate will sure be happy if you stay."

Would he? They had been back together almost a month now and he still refused to discuss the future.

"Cody, too," Mel said. "I think he has a crush on you."

Cait smiled. Cody was an awesome kid. She knew without a doubt that despite his disability, he was destined for great things. With parents as involved as Nate and Mel, how could he not be? "The feeling is mutual," she told Mel. She just hoped Cody's affection for her didn't falter when he learned that she was more than Daddy's friend. Cody loved his dad, but deep down he was a mama's boy. He and Mel had a strong bond, and Caitie hoped he wouldn't see her as an interloper.

So far so good.

"It probably wouldn't be the kind of money that you're used to," Mel said. "Not at first anyway."

"It's not just about the money. Not in the way that you might think. I just need the security of a regular paycheck and a little money in savings for emergencies. I need a whole lot less money here than if I were still in New York. But more than anything, I need to feel useful. As if I'm accomplishing something and bettering myself. I like helping people."

"Owning a business is hard work," Mel said. "Which you know from watching your parents run the diner. At times it can be downright scary. Especially when you have employees who count on you for their job security. But the sense of accomplishment you feel is worth it. Sometimes at night when everyone is gone and I'm closing up, I'll stop and just look around the salon and think, I *own* this. This is *mine*. I did it all by myself."

"You realized your dream. A lot of people never get there. And sometimes the ones who do find it's not what they expected."

Mel eyed her curiously. "Are you speaking from experience?"

"Let's just say that I'm seeing things a bit differently now."

"What things?"

"I worked hard and sacrificed so much to build my career. I *thought* I was happy, but, looking back, I realize that I barely had a life. I was too busy and too focused to realize what I was missing, that there was more to life than climbing the ladder of success."

"There's nothing wrong with wanting to be successful," Mel said. "I think what it's really about is knowing when to draw the line. When determination becomes obsession. When you lose sight of what is truly important."

"Priorities," Caitie said.

"Exactly! I love my job, but absolutely nothing compares to the gratification of raising a child. He's my number one priority."

That was exactly what Caitie needed to do. Assess her priorities. Did she want to work eighty-hour weeks to afford that fully loaded luxury car she'd had her eye on, or drive the much cheaper compact and have time to spend with her family? Did she want to be one of those women who were so obsessed with success that they had no life? No friends.

"By the way, I forgot to mention that your mom made a hair appointment for next week," Mel said.

"She's been complaining about her gray roots for weeks." Now if she could just remember the appointment. "Remember, she doesn't know that you know."

"Mum's the word."

One of the stylists appeared in the office doorway. "Mel, your three o'clock is here."

"You want to take her to the bowl and get her ready?"

"Sure."

When she was gone, Caitie told Mel, "I have to go anyway. I need to stop by the diner. Then I have a ton of research to do if I'm going to seriously consider this." Nate was working a double shift, so she was on her own for the night.

"I hope you do. Remember when we were younger and we used to talk about the future? How we would both get married and live in Paradise so our kids could be best friends, too. But this is even better. If you and Nate have a baby, they'll be siblings."

Caitie wasn't sure if she was ready to have a baby just yet, but it was definitely in the cards.

They hugged goodbye and made tentative plans for the weekend.

Cait's parents were in Denver for her mom's monthly checkup at her neurologist, and a trip to the restaurant supply, and wouldn't be home until late, so she had the house to herself. She made herself a sandwich, popped a beer, shut her phone off and got to work. With all the resources available online, it didn't take her long to realize that starting her own company wasn't just feasible; it would be fairly simple. Even better, when she packed it in at nine and turned her phone back on, representatives from five local businesses had left her messages. At this rate, she would be up and running in no time.

She felt a giddy sort of lightness all the way through to her soul. An entire world had just opened up to her, a whole new set of opportunities. It was a little intimidating, but exciting, too, and she was ready to reach out and grab it. And she couldn't wait to tell Nate.

She was too excited to sleep, to even sit for more than a minute or two, so she grabbed a notepad and began to list all the things she would have to do to make the transition. She would have to call her landlord and tell him that she wouldn't be renewing her lease—which was conveniently up next month. Maybe the girl subletting would be interested in staying there permanently.

Caitie would have to plan a trip to New York to pick up the things from her apartment that she wanted to keep. Although admittedly there wasn't much. Most of what she had were just *things*. Conveniences that she had little emotional attachment to. Anything she had that was special to her, she'd brought with her to Paradise. Maybe going back wasn't necessary after all.

Caitie crawled into bed around eleven-thirty. She heard her parents come in about fifteen minutes later. As excited as she was, she resisted the urge to get back out of bed and give them the good news. Of course she wanted them to know, but she wanted Nate to be the first person she told since one of her main reasons for staying was him.

She must have dozed off at some point, because the next thing she knew, she was being shaken awake. She opened her eyes, expecting to see one of her parents, but it was Nate leaning over her bed. It was dark, but she could see that he was still in his uniform. She peered over at the clock and saw that it was almost 1:00 a.m., meaning he was still on duty.

"Caitie, wake up," he said.

She groaned and rolled over onto her stomach, too tired to hold her eyes open, and mumbled, "If you're here for a quickie, you're in for a major disappointment."

"You have to wake up," he said, gently rubbing her back, which did nothing to help his cause. She could feel herself drifting back to sleep.

"I brought you something," he said.

"Can you give it to me tomorrow?"

"I see you're just as stubborn as ever," a female voice said. A very *familiar* female voice.

Caitie rolled back over and sat up. *"Kelly?"*

Nate switched on the lamp beside the bed, and sure enough it was Kelly standing behind him, dressed in skinny jeans and a clingy sweater that accentuated her pinup figure. Her long, sleek blond hair hung loose over her shoulders and draped down to cover most of the left side of her face. She looked daring and mysterious and gorgeous as always, and Caitie felt that familiar twinge of envy.

"I left you a dozen messages," Caitie told her.

"I know. And I'm sorry I didn't call back."

"Where the hell have you been?"

"Europe. My phone didn't work there."

"*Europe?* What the hell were you doing there?"

"I was with my fian—" She stopped, correcting herself. "Make that ex-fiancé."

"You're *engaged?*"

"*Was* engaged. Until he did this." She brushed the hair back off her face and Caitie gasped. She had an angry-looking purplish-blue bruise that ran from the outer corner of her eye—which was swollen almost shut—down to her jaw.

"He *hit* you?"

"Don't worry—he's in way worse shape than me."

Nate cleared his throat and tapped the face of his watch.

"Yeah, I know," Kelly said. Then she told Caitie, "I'll explain it later, after you post my bond."

Caitie was sure she'd heard her wrong. "Did you just say bond?"

"I pulled her over just outside of town," Nate said. "For doing twenty over."

Caitie blinked. "You arrested her for that?"

"I arrested her for the stolen vehicle she was driving."

Chapter Fifteen

Out of courtesy and a bit of sentimentality, and because she promised to behave, Nate waited until they
were back outside to cuff Kelly. Caitie wanted to go
with them, but there was really no point. Until Kelly
was arraigned in the morning, there was nothing anyone could do.

When they got to the station, he booked her and
locked her in a holding cell, then went to get her an ice
pack. She winced as she pressed it to her face.

"Are you sure you don't want me to call a doctor?"
Nate asked her.

"It's just a bruise," she said. "Nothing broken."

"Let me know if you change your mind."

"So, Deputy, I couldn't help noticing that you
looked awfully comfortable in my sister's bedroom."

"You'll have to talk to your sister about that."

"A gentleman never kisses and tells?" she said, and for an instant she looked just like Caitie. But that was where any similarity stopped.

"Something like that," he told her. Back when he was dating Caitie, Kelly had never passed up an opportunity to make a pest of herself. So, of course, after he'd earned his badge, he'd been more than happy to return the favor. And she made it all too easy. As a kid she was a pain in the ass, but in high school she had been downright out of control. He lost count of how many times he'd dragged her out of trouble. *Literally* dragged. At times in handcuffs. But he never had the heart to book her, though looking back, it may have been just what she needed to scare her straight.

Kelly must have read his mind. "You know, after Caitie left for school, when pretty much everyone else had given up on me, you were there, riding my ass, keeping me out of trouble."

"It was my job."

"Yes, but that isn't why you did it."

No, it wasn't. He knew about regret and missed chances and the cruelty of fate. It had been obvious to him that she was hurting and confused. And he knew that under the bravado and attitude there was a good kid.

"Knowing you cared is probably the only thing that kept me from crossing the line, from doing something really stupid. And I never thanked you. Never told you how much it meant to me."

"You just did."

Kelly smiled. "She's lucky to have you."

"No, I'm the lucky one. Is there anything else you need before I go?"

"A metal file?"

He grinned in spite of himself. "I'll see you to-morrow."

"Hey, Deputy," she said. "Thanks for tonight."

"For arresting you?"

"For *believing* me. I know you could get in trouble for taking me home first."

"Try to get some sleep," he said, switching the light off as he walked out. Leave it to Kelly to get herself into this crazy mess.

He'd promised Caitie that he would come back after Kelly was processed, and when he got there, despite it being two-thirty in the morning, she was wide-awake and waiting for him in the kitchen.

"How is she?" Caitie asked the instant he stepped through the door.

"She's Kelly," he said, unbuttoning his cuffs, and Caitie nodded, as if that was explanation enough.

"What did she say happened?"

"Can we have this conversation in bed? I'm beat."

"Sure. Of course."

Preferably he would like to have it in the morning after a couple hours of sleep and a big cup of black coffee, but if it were his sibling, he would feel the same way. Even a sibling who had caused as much grief to the family as Kelly had.

The call from the L.A. precinct had come in the early afternoon, and Nate had been patrolling the borders of the city, watching for Kelly for the rest of the day. For her family's sake, he wanted to be the one to apprehend her.

Caitie was already in her pajamas, so she climbed

right into bed. Nate stripped down to his boxers and slipped in beside her.

Looking anxious, Caitie said, "So, what did she tell you?"

"The guy's name is David Sparks. Young, independently wealthy, hot as hell—her words, not mine. They had a whirlwind affair that resulted in him proposing in Europe."

"How long has she known him?"

"I'm guessing not long. She said after he proposed he started acting strange. Real possessive. If another man would even look at her, he would go off. When they got back to the States, she checked her phone and got your messages. She told him what was happening with your mom, and that she had to go home for a while. He told her that he needed her there and that she couldn't go."

"I can just imagine how well that went over," Caitie said.

"She told him, yes, she was going, and he said no, you aren't, and she said try and stop me, so he belted her."

"What did she do?"

"Waited until his back was turned and clobbered him with an empty wine bottle."

Caitie winced. "Ouch."

"Yeah, she knocked him out cold. Gave him a concussion. While he was unconscious, she grabbed a few things, hopped into his car and took off. When he came to, he called the police."

"What's going to happen to her?"

"I'm betting that when he's had time to cool down,

he'll drop the charges. This isn't his first physical altercation with a girlfriend."

"She sure does know how to pick 'em," Caitie said. "Maybe she'll learn this time."

Somehow he doubted that. "I grabbed her bag out of the car before it was impounded. It's in my truck."

"Thank you."

He yawned, his lids drooping. "Can we go to sleep now?"

She hesitated, chewing her lip.

"What?" he asked her.

She smiled. "There was something I wanted to tell you, but it can wait until tomorrow."

"Good, because I'm beat." So beat that he was out before his head hit the pillow.

As Nate had predicted, after being showed photos of Kelly's injuries, Mr. Sparks reluctantly dropped the charges. No one was more relieved than Caitie's parents, and Kelly swore to them that the experience had been a much-needed wake-up call. Nate would believe that when he saw it.

Knowing they would need some family time, just the four of them, he made himself scarce. He had the day off, and Cody only had a half day of school, so they drove to Boulder for lunch and school clothes shopping. Cody had grown three inches over the summer. Not only did he tower over most of his classmates, but the new jeans Mel had picked up for him last month were rapidly becoming floods.

They stopped for lunch at Cody's favorite fast-food place, and out of the blue Cody asked him, "Dad, why is Grandma Phillips mad at Caitie?"

He stopped short of rolling his eyes. Mel's mom was always upset with somebody about something, but, as much as he disliked her, she was still Cody's grandmother. He treated her with respect, even though she hadn't exactly earned it. Mel and her mom had been at odds pretty much since Mel emerged from the womb. For reasons Nate never understood, his ex-mother-in-law prided herself on her ability to tear Mel down and crush her self-esteem, and for some reason Mel took it. She gave her mom too much power. Someday something was going to give. Mel would reach her limit, and Nate hoped he wasn't around for the explosion that would follow.

"What makes you think she's mad at her?" he asked Cody.

Cody shrugged.

Nate didn't want to interrogate his own son, but he needed to know what was going on. "Did your grandma say something about Caitie?"

"She called her a bad name."

His jaw tensed. It wouldn't be the first time she'd behaved inappropriately in front of his son. If she kept it up, they would have to have a "talk" about what was and wasn't appropriate to say in front of a six-year-old. Just like he'd had to explain to her that it wasn't appropriate to let Cody stay up until 3:00 a.m. watching R-rated movies with explicit violence and language. But thankfully it was a rare occasion that he spent the night at her place. She liked to label herself the "fun" grandma, and had once accused Nate's mom of being too "uptight."

"Grandma shouldn't use bad language," he told Cody.

"Why is she so mean to Mommy?"

"I wish I knew, Cody." Mel's mom had always favored her son, who was two years younger than Mel. Nate's theory was that Mel's mom saw her not as her daughter but as competition.

"Is Caitie your girlfriend?" Cody asked him.

Oh boy, there it was. *The* question. "Would it bother you if I had a girlfriend?"

"No."

He took a chance and asked, "What if I got married again? Would that bother you?"

"Would you marry Caitie?"

He nodded.

"Would I have to call her Mom?"

He stifled a grin. "I think it would be better if you just called her Caitie."

"Will Mom be sad if you marry someone else?"

"You know that your mom and I love each other. But not like a married couple. We're friends. Kind of like you and Lily Ann are friends."

"Do you love Caitie?"

The depth of Cody's curiosity, and his logical way of approaching matters, never ceased to amaze Nate. "I do love Caitie, but that doesn't mean I love your mom, or you, any less. You know that, right?"

"I know."

"My grandma used to tell me that the more people you love, the bigger your heart gets."

An eye roll from Cody seemed to suggest that he was already privy to that information. "Would you and Caitie have a baby?"

He hoped so. He hoped she would be open to having two or three, but they were getting way ahead of themselves. For all he knew, she was still planning to go back to New York.

"We'll just have to wait and see," he told Cody.

They both would.

He managed to get Cody home by his bedtime and helped tuck him in. He warned Mel that her mom was up to her old tricks, and she promised to have a talk with her.

He hadn't heard from Caitie all day, and, assuming she was busy with family matters, he drove straight home. He had just settled on the couch with a beer and was about to turn on the football game he'd DVR'd Monday night, when someone knocked on his front door.

It was Caitie.

"How did it go with Kelly?" he asked as she took her jacket off and made herself comfortable on the couch beside him.

"Well, she's decided to stay for a while, since she basically has nowhere else to go. And since she doesn't have a job, she'll have plenty of time to help with our mom. Which will be a big help now that I *do* have a job."

His heart dropped, then shot back up and lodged in his throat. "You heard from your headhunter?"

"No, but, thanks to Mel, I've discovered that a lot of businesses in town are pretty desperate for a reliable bookkeeper, and I've decided to start my own company."

Suddenly it was difficult to breathe. "Here in Paradise?"

"I've had a dozen calls already and I haven't even printed up business cards."

He tried not to get his hopes up just yet. For all he knew this could be something she planned to do only until something better came along.

"I've hit a bit of a snag though," she said, and his hope plummeted. "I was planning to make a temporary office in my parents' den, but now that Kelly is back she'll be sleeping in there." She hesitated. "I know it's a lot to ask, because you're tight on space, too, but I thought maybe you would be willing to spare me a corner of your living room so I can set up a workspace. Just until I have enough of a cash flow to rent an office."

"That might be doable," he said, trying not to get his hopes up.

"Or we could rent a bigger place. A three bedroom, so I would have a home office."

"We? You're talking about moving in together?"

"I know we've only been back together a month—"

"Hold on," he said, needing clarification before they went any further. "How long do you see yourself having this business?"

"If all goes as planned, the next thirty years or so."

His heart skipped a beat. "That's a long time."

"I know you've been hesitant to discuss the future, and I can't blame you for that, but I can't live in limbo any longer. I need to know what I'm doing with the rest of my life. And I need to know if you want to be in it."

Did he ever. He pulled Caitie close, feeling as if his life, the life he had always wanted, was finally coming together. And it was about damn time. "I most definitely want to be in it."

"I wasn't sure. I could tell that you've been holding back…."

"Then let me be perfectly clear," he said, cupping her face in his hands. "I love you. I want to spend the rest of my life with you. I just needed to know that you feel that way, too, and that you'd come to that conclusion without any coercion from me." He'd made that mistake once before, assuming she wanted the same things he did.

Caitie kissed him, pressed her forehead to his. "I love you, Nathan."

"I know."

"It used to scare me to death how much I needed you."

"Caitie, you never needed me."

"No, I did. Desperately. Sometimes I felt so alone. So…invisible."

"I always saw you. I guess I just wasn't all that great about showing it." But not anymore. If it meant telling her that he loved her a hundred times a day, that's what he would do to assure her that she was the only one for him.

"It may have taken me seven years to figure it out, but this is home. Being in Paradise with you. And when I look back on the last few years of my life, I can't help but wonder, what was I thinking? The person I was there, the person I was becoming…that just isn't me anymore. Maybe it never was."

As far as he was concerned, the past was past. She was here now, and that was all that really mattered.

Chapter Sixteen

Caitie stood outside Joe's Place, willing herself to step inside, feeling more nervous than she had in her whole life. Since moving back to Paradise, Caitie had seen P.J., Nate's dad, at the diner several times, but she had yet to run into his mom, Lynn. Now that Caitie and Nate were officially together, not to mention house hunting, she knew she would have to face Lynn sooner or later. Lynn apparently shared the sentiment because she had called and asked Caitie out to lunch, said she had avoided her long enough.

She could only imagine how much Lynn probably hated her after what Caitie had done to her son. She and P.J. had always been so kind to Caitie, made her feel welcome, as if she were already a part of their family. By leaving she had betrayed them, too.

Since the idea of having a mother-in-law who hated

her sucked big-time, she was determined to patch things up. To earn her way back into Lynn's good graces, and, if she was lucky, maybe someday into her heart.

It was now or never.

Caitie pushed her way through the door, stopping to let her eyes adjust to the dark interior. Lynn sat at a booth right up front by the window. She must have come straight over from work, because she was wearing her postal uniform. Caitie forced her feet to carry her there, and she had a speech all prepared, but as she reached the table, she couldn't think of a single thing to say. She doubted if she could even articulate anything with all the breath backing up in her lungs.

Lynn stood to greet her. "Long time no see," she said.

"Hi. How are you?"

"Tired of waiting around for you to come say hello."

"Honestly, I didn't think you would ever want to see me again after what I had done to Nate."

"Well, you were wrong." Lynn smiled and held out her arms. "Now come here and give me a hug."

Tears burning the backs of her eyes, Caitie stepped into her arms. Lynn hugged her so hard she could barely breathe and the blood that had begun to pool in her lower extremities rushed back up to Caitie's brain.

"I'm so sorry that I hurt Nate. That I hurt you and P.J."

Lynn held her at arm's length. "You were a confused kid making adult decisions. The important thing is that you're back. To stay."

"Yes, definitely," she said.

"Why don't we sit down? I only have forty-five minutes, and we have a lot to talk about."

Caitie hoped it was all good things.

"Are you hungry?" Lynn asked her. "Lunch is on me."

"Sure," Caitie said, even though her stomach was so tied in knots she couldn't imagine being able to choke anything down.

Lynn signaled for the waitress, and they put in their orders.

"So, first things first," Lynn said. "Tell me how your mom is doing. I hope you don't mind that Nate told me about her condition."

"No, of course not. She's…okay. She has good days and bad days."

"Nate said there have been a few incidents."

"Since Kelly has been back, things have been going much more smoothly. For lack of a better term, she's become my mom's full-time caretaker. As you can imagine, the fact that Kelly is willing to help at all is a miracle in itself. And it's given me time to concentrate on getting my business going."

"Is there anything I can do for your mom? I want to help somehow."

"What she really needs is company. Someone to talk to. I think she's lonely." How could she not be? Yes, Kelly was there, but that wasn't the same as seeing her friends.

"I would love to see her," Lynn said. "Should I call first?"

"Honestly, it would be better if you just showed up. Otherwise she would probably tell you not to come. I think she's embarrassed."

"We'll fix that," Lynn said, with the same look of unwavering determination she had seen a million times on Nate's face. "For years your mom has taken care of the people in this town. Her friends will want to be there in her time of need."

The thought nearly brought tears to Caitie's eyes. "That's what we keep telling her."

"Then shame on her for not believing it."

Caitie's cell phone rang, and she checked the display. It was a local number but not a familiar one. Probably someone else looking for a new bookkeeper.

"Do you mind if I take this?" she asked Lynn. "It might be a potential client. I just want to tell them that I'll call back later."

"Of course, honey. Go ahead."

It was Melinda Price, the sheriff's secretary. "Sweetie, have you heard from your dad?"

Cait's adrenaline instantly went into overdrive, and her heart sank to her knees. Lynn must have seen it in her face, because she sat up straighter.

"I'm not sure where he is. Why?"

"We've been trying to locate him. Your mom is here at the station."

The blood in Caitie's veins turned to ice. "Why? Is she okay?"

"Fine, honey, just fine, but she's very confused. There was an incident at the thrift store. Can you come down here?"

"Of course." Thank goodness she was okay. She must have gotten lost, though she was supposed to be under Kelly's supervision today. "I'll be right there."

Caitie grabbed her keys and purse and told Lynn, "I have to go."

"I'm not letting you behind the wheel like this," Lynn said, and Caitie realized that she was trembling. "I'll drive you."

On the way there, Caitie called her sister. She answered on the first ring.

"Yello!"

"Where the hell are you?" Caitie demanded, her voice trembling with fear and rage.

"A-at Rene's house. Caitie, what's wrong?"

"Mom is at the police station. So I ask again, *where the hell are you?* You're supposed to be with her!"

"I thought she was at the salon."

"Apparently she isn't."

"Oh my God, I'll be right there."

Caitie hung up and called her dad, but it went directly to voice mail. He had a habit of forgetting to turn his cell phone on. She left a message, hoping he would hear it soon.

"Would you like me to go inside with you?" Lynn asked when they got to the station.

"I think it might embarrass her. But I appreciate the offer."

Lynn dropped her off out front, and it was Nate who met Caitie at the door. It was his day off, and he was dressed in jeans and a lavender polo. He was one of the few guys she'd ever known who could look macho in pastel.

"She's okay," he assured her, but in reality, she wasn't. Caitie had a feeling that this was only a sneak peek at what was in store for them for the future. She was only going to get worse.

"Where is she?"

"In the sheriff's office. He's calming her down."

The door swung open, and Kelly rushed in looking frantic, her makeup smeared, eyes red from crying. "Is she okay?"

"She's safe now," Caitie said. "Nate was just about to tell me what happened."

"I'm not one hundred percent sure," he said. "She's still very confused. From what I understand, she was at the thrift store and one of the employees saw her stick something in her purse."

Caitie could hardly believe what she was hearing. "Are you saying that she was caught *shoplifting?*"

"It looks that way. When she tried to leave, they stopped her at the door and pulled a scarf out of her purse. According to the clerk, she got very belligerent, insisted it was hers even though the tags were still on it. They called the police."

"Why weren't you with her?" Caitie asked, turning to her sister. Kelly flinched at her sharp tone.

"I dropped her off at the salon for her appointment. I offered to stay with her. I tried to, but she said something about not being a total invalid yet and to stop treating her like a damned child. She actually snapped at me."

"So you just left her there? I specifically asked you to stay there with her, didn't I?"

She bit her lip and nodded. "I screwed up. I'm sorry. I don't know what else to say. She was supposed to call me when she was done."

"There's no way she could have finished that quickly," Caitie said.

Nate pulled out his cell phone. "I'll call Mel. Maybe she'll know what happened."

When Mel answered, Nate explained the confusion,

listened for a minute, then said, "I see." He handed the phone to Caitie. "She wants to talk to you."

Caitie took the phone from him. "Hey, Mel."

"Oh, Caitie, I am so sorry."

"What happened? Wasn't she supposed to get her hair done?"

"A cut and color. But I was running about fifteen minutes late. She said she was going to run down to the thrift store real quick. She seemed so lucid and cheerful, like her old self. I didn't think anything of it. But when she didn't come back, I started to worry. I was getting ready to call you when Nate called me. Is she okay?"

"Nate said she's fine. I haven't talked to her yet."

"I feel awful. I never should have let her leave. If there's anything I can do…"

"I just want to get her home."

"I'm here if you need me. Give your mom my best."

After she hung up with Mel, she handed back Nate's phone and asked, "Are they going to press charges?"

"They were, until I explained the situation."

Her mom's time of hiding the disease was officially over.

The door opened again, but this time it was her dad who rushed in, his face pale, a sheen of sweat beading his forehead, as if he'd sprinted there from wherever he'd been. "Where is she?"

"In with the sheriff," Nate told him; then he repeated what he had told Caitie and Kelly.

"Is she under arrest?" her dad asked.

Nate shook his head. "I smoothed things over with the manager."

The look her father shot Kelly could have curdled milk. "I thought you were supposed to be with her."

Kelly looked so devastated that Caitie heard herself defending her sister. "She told Kelly it was okay to leave. You know how persuasive she can be."

"Next time you tell her no. You're staying. Period."

"Put yourself in our place," Caitie replied. "We grew up having to do what she told us. It's difficult to turn that around." Although in fairness to her dad, Kelly defied them on a daily basis. Why would he trust her to do the right thing now? She was going to have to prove herself, to earn his trust.

"I'd like you girls to go," Lou said. "This will be embarrassing enough for her without an audience. And I don't want either of you to mention this to her."

"Maybe it would be good for her to talk about it," Caitie said. "To come to terms with it."

"I know what's best for my wife," he said firmly, looking so beside himself Caitie's heart broke for him. "Go back to whatever you were doing, and when you come home later, just act as if you know nothing about it."

"We'll do that," Caitie assured him, and Kelly agreed. Caitie wasn't sure if this was a constructive approach to the problem, but he knew her better than anyone. She and Kelly would have to trust his judgment.

What other choice did they have?

"Go on back to the sheriff's office, Lou," Nate told her dad. "They're waiting for you."

"I'll see you girls at home later." He gave Caitie and her sister a hug, and he was so tense, so brittle with worry, Caitie was afraid for him. Afraid of what the stress was doing to his health. He used to be so laid-back and easygoing. But lately he'd been constantly on edge. Caitie could hardly recall the last time that he'd cracked a smile. This was tearing him apart, one little piece at a time.

Caitie, Kelly and Nate left the station together and walked to the parking lot in the back, where Kelly had parked.

"I have my reservations about this," Kelly said as they stopped beside the car. "I'm afraid it might harm more than help her."

"We have to trust that Dad knows what he's doing. If she wants us to know, she'll tell us. And next time you take her to the salon, stay with her."

Tears pooled in Kelly's eyes. "I will. I'm so sorry, Caitie. If I had known this would happen, I never would have left her."

"The point is that you *did* leave her."

Kelly nodded, the tears rolling down her cheeks, and Caitie fought back a wave of sympathy. What Kelly needed was tough love.

Kelly brushed the tears away with the back of her hand. "I've been trying really hard not to screw up."

"Try harder. The next time someone could end up hurt. Or worse."

"It won't happen again."

Caitie turned to Nate. "Could you give me a lift to Joe's Place? I left my car there." She could walk, but word about what happened had probably already gotten around. There would be a lot of curious looks and questions that she was in no mood to answer.

"Of course," Nate said. "I'm parked across the street."

She said goodbye to Kelly, who was still crying, and they walked to Nate's truck.

"Don't you think you were a little hard on her?" he asked Caitie. "It sounded like an honest mistake."

"That honest mistake could have gotten my mother killed. On her way to the thrift store she could have forgotten to look both ways and gotten mowed down by a car. Or what if the store manager hadn't been so understanding and pressed charges? She could be sitting in a jail cell right now. And I don't have to tell you how expensive a good defense can be."

"I guess I see your point." He opened the passenger's side door for her, then walked around and got in. "I don't know if now is a good time for this, but I had an idea I wanted to run past you."

"Okay."

He started the engine and pulled out into traffic. "I wondered how you would feel about instead of renting or even buying a house, what if we built new?"

It was an option she hadn't even considered. They had seen a few houses already, and so far she hadn't been impressed. "Interesting idea."

"That way we would be getting exactly what we need."

"But we would have to find property somewhere."

"Maybe not." He stopped for a red light and turned to her. "How do you think your parents would feel about splitting their lot and letting us build on it? That way, if your mom needed you, you would only be a short walk away. Kelly is there now, but at some point she's going to want a life of her own. Your mom would be so close, she could come to our house and you could keep an eye on her there."

Hearing him say *our house* gave her a shiver of pleasure. "If we present it to them that way, I doubt they would say no. But are you sure that's something you'd be willing to do?"

He pulled into the lot at Joe's Place and parked beside her car. He cut the engine and turned to her. "I'm not sure what you mean."

"You'd be willing to live so close to my parents?"

"It's not as if we would be in the same house. If it were my mom who was sick, wouldn't you be willing to do the same for her?"

"Without a doubt."

"Family is family. We may find ourselves in the same situation someday, with our kids taking care of us. That's the way it's supposed to work."

"Our kids," she said with a smile. "I like the sound of that."

"Why don't we give your parents a couple of days and ask them about it."

Chapter Seventeen

As Nate suspected, after they explained their reasoning, Caitie's parents were thrilled with the idea of them building on the property. And after combing the internet for several days, they finally decided on an architectural firm in Boulder. On Nate's next day off, they hopped in his truck and headed out to meet the architect.

On the way there, Caitie pulled out a pen and notepad and they made a list of what each would want and need in a home. Thirty seconds into the conversation, Nate was convinced that Caitie had either developed a seriously warped sense of humor or completely lost her mind.

She claimed that they needed at least *four thousand* square feet that included four bedrooms, each with an en-suite bath, an enormous eat-in kitchen and formal dining room, a great room with a stone fireplace and cathedral ceiling and finally, a spacious office to run her business. Add to that the three-car attached garage he was hoping for, and what they were describing was nothing short of a mini-mansion.

"Do we really need a home that large?" he asked her.

"I never thought I would hear myself say this," she told him, "but this land has been in my family for generations. This is our forever home. If we're going to spend the rest of our lives here, shouldn't we build the home that we really want?"

Wanting something didn't mean it was practical. Or even conceivable. "I understand how you feel, but is it really worth being house poor, with an enormous mortgage?"

"Not at all. That's why we're going to pay cash."

Nate's grip on the steering wheel went rigid and his heart sank in his chest. *Cash?* Was she serious?

He made decent money for a small town deputy, and had a little in savings, but not enough to pay cash for a new house. "I'm not sure how realistic a goal that is," he told her.

"I have a little money put away that I'd been planning to spend on an apartment in Manhattan. It will go ten times further here than it would have in New York."

"When you say a little money, how little are we talking?"

When she gave him the sum, he nearly swallowed his own tongue. She didn't have a "little" money saved. She had a small fortune. It was to him anyway. Enough to buy their mini-mansion and furnish it with plenty to spare.

He knew that she'd made good money in New York, he just hadn't realized *how* good. The subject had never come up, and honestly he'd never given it much thought. He never imagined it would matter. But now he found himself intimidated by her success. By her *potential*. Did she truly realize what she would be giving up by staying in Paradise with him? By starting her own business instead of holding out for a position in a large firm? All that hard work, all those years of college earning her degree, and she was just going to give it all up? For him?

He was a cop. It was all he ever wanted to do, and he loved it, but it wouldn't be making him rich. Not even close. That had never been a problem for him. But now he couldn't help questioning if that might someday become a problem for her.

She claimed that she used to think she wasn't good enough for him. Maybe what it boiled down to was that *he* wasn't good enough for *her*. Maybe he never had been, and he was fooling himself into thinking this relationship had a chance in hell of surviving. And as he watched her write out a check and hand it over to the architect, he had to fight an impending sense of doom. But if Caitie noticed, she said nothing about it.

Self-doubt gnawed away at Nate for days, and he found himself questioning his own worth, until he was convinced that Caitie was settling for a life that would never make her truly happy.

The following week they drove back to Boulder to look at the preliminary plans, which Nathan couldn't deny were close to perfect. The budget on the other hand, nearly made him lose his lunch.

They left with a copy of the plans in hand, and Cait insisted they stop by first his parents' house, then hers. And when his dad made what was supposed to be a joke about Nate being a "kept man," he couldn't help but wonder if his dad was right.

They were about five minutes from home when Caitie, who had been checking her email on her phone, mumbled something he didn't catch.

"What was that?" he said.

She stuck her phone back in her purse. "I said, it freaking figures."

"What figures?"

"I just got an email from my headhunter. He got me an interview."

Nate's heart slammed into the wall of his chest. He hadn't been aware that she was still looking.

"Where?" he asked, expecting her to name a town somewhat close by, like Boulder or Denver.

"In New York, if you can believe that," she said. "I don't suppose you'd like to take an overnight trip with me. I do have a few things in storage that I'd like to pick up anyway. I could kill two birds."

His grip tightened on the wheel and his head spun until the road went blurry. *Two* birds? "Are you saying that you want to go to the interview?"

"As a professional courtesy, I probably should. He worked really hard to find this."

Jesus, it was starting already. "Why was he still looking? Didn't you tell him that you were starting your own business?"

"To be honest, it hadn't even crossed my mind. It had been so long since I'd heard from him, I figured he'd given up on me."

Or she wanted him to keep looking, just in case. "It just seems odd that you wouldn't call and tell him to stop looking," he pressed. "Seems like a pretty major waste of his time."

"I know. And I feel terrible for it. Which is why I feel I have to go. He said that he had to call in a couple favors to get this interview. Not going would be a slap in the face. I may need him someday."

"For what?"

She shrugged. "Who knows? But I've learned to never burn bridges. It's bad business." She paused, then said, "So what do you think? Would you want to go? Cody could even come with us, though he might have to miss a day or two of school. Unless I can schedule the interview for late on a Friday afternoon. Then we could stay the whole weekend. The city is gorgeous in the fall."

Though it was difficult, he kept his eyes on the road, the yellow line undulating in front of him. "And if you decided you want it?"

"Want what?"

"The job. Are Cody and I just supposed to leave you there? Ship your things back to you from Paradise?"

She blinked in confusion. "But…I *don't* want the job."

"You may change your mind after you hear what they're offering."

She shifted in her seat. "Okay, what the hell is going on? You've been in a rotten mood all day. This is supposed to be fun. Building a house together, planning for our future. It's supposed to be exciting."

How big of a fool did she take him for?

"Why don't you just admit it," he said, so angry his voice shook.

"Admit *what?*"

"That you want the job."

"But I *don't* want the job."

"If you go to the interview and turn them down, does your headhunter still get paid?"

"No, but that's not the point."

"Maybe it should be."

"My reputation is important to me."

"That's what it always seems to boil down to," he said. "What's important to *you.*"

"Nathan, what is going on? Why are you acting this way?"

"Why don't you admit what this really is," he said, blinking as the lines in the road began to blur. "Your fear of commitment. You want to be with me, as long as you can keep me at a comfortable distance. Just like you did in high school. I don't think that your leaving had anything to do with you thinking I was too good for you. What you really thought is that you were too good for me."

"Oh my God. Nathan…" She shook her head. "Where is this coming from?"

"Do you deny it?"

"Yes, as a matter of fact, I do. Vehemently. Because what you're saying is just…*crazy.* I don't want to live in New York, or any other big city for that matter. I'm happy here, with you."

She thought so now, but how would she feel when they made her an offer and she saw all those zeros? "You need an escape plan."

"No! That's not it at all."

"What we have here together…it's never going to be enough for you."

"But it already is enough. I swear. I love you. I want to be with you."

"I wish I could believe that. But obviously I can't give you what you need."

"And what is it that you think I need?"

"A big house, expensive cars…whatever. I'm a cop, and I'm always going to be a cop."

He glanced over at her, and she was staring at him, her mouth agape. "Is that what this is about? *Money?*"

"I love you, Caitie. It's always been you. I want to start a life with you. Spend the rest of my life with you. But not if I'm going to have to spend the next fifty years chasing you down."

"What are you saying?"

Something he never thought he would hear himself say. He wasn't one to issue ultimatums, but he'd run out of options. "Either you're in or you're out. You're with me or you're not. There's no more halfway."

Caitie blinked. "Are you breaking up with me?"

"I don't know, am I? The ball is in your court. Feel free to call me when you make up your mind. But don't expect me to wait another seven years."

"Wow," she said, shaking her head again, looking shell-shocked. "Just…wow."

He made a too-sharp turn into his driveway, shoved the gear into Park, and for several minutes they just sat there, neither saying a word.

This was it, he thought. This was really the end. It wasn't as if he'd been pining for her the past seven years, but somewhere in the back of his mind he had never completely lost hope that they might someday be together.

"I honestly thought it would be a fun trip," she finally said, "but if it's that big of a problem for you, forget it."

"Forget what?"

"The trip to New York, the interview. It's not worth it if it's going to break us up. And, by the way, if you want to talk about having intimacy issues, take a good hard look in the mirror first. Because I am definitely not the one keeping people at arm's length in this particular scenario."

He eyed her suspiciously. Was she using reverse psychology on him? Telling him she didn't want to go so he would then tell her it was okay? "So, now you're saying you're *not* going to go?"

"Not if it's going to upset you. I can arrange to have my things shipped back to me."

"What about your headhunter?"

"I'll tell him the truth. That I forgot to call him, and I've decided to stay here. That I'm in love—though it would seem that you're not ready to believe it. I guess we'll just have to work on that."

He blinked. "So you aren't going."

She blew out a frustrated breath. "I'm *not* going. Not now, not ever. Period."

He didn't know what to say. He wasn't even sure what to think. Or what he *had* been thinking. Was he really so insecure that he would throw away what they had over something as stupid as money? Why didn't he just come right out and accuse her of being shallow and insensitive?

Why? Because she was neither of those things.

He had just given the world's stupidest ultimatum to the woman he had been in love with for the better part of the past eight years. What the hell was he thinking?

Dumbfounded by his own stupidity, he reached for Caitie, knowing full well that if she turned him away, he completely deserved it. But she didn't do that. She fell into his arms instead, burrowed her face into the crook of his neck.

"Caitie, I'm so sorry. I don't know what I was thinking."

"Me, neither," she said, squeezing him so tight. "I could tell that something was bothering you this past week. I figured that you would talk about it when you were ready."

He'd just come frighteningly close to throwing away the best thing that had ever happened to him, and for what? Pride? Because she made more money than he did? *Jesus.* "I'm an idiot."

"You're not going to get an argument from me. Next time, instead of freaking out and making wild assumptions, why don't you try just talking to me, telling me how you feel. You and Mel managed to maintain a friendship through a pretty lousy situation by communicating. By telling each other how you feel. Can't we do that, too? Can we be lovers and friends?"

"You're right," he said, kissing her forehead, her cheeks. "I'm so sorry. I have no excuse. I was wrong. It was just my stupid pride. I want to take care of you. Give you anything you could possibly want. But knowing how much money you made..."

She caught his face in her hands, smiling up at him, when what she should have done was punch him in the nose for being such a moron. "You've already given me what I want. *You*. And as for taking care of me, why don't we take care of each other instead?"

He had never been so relieved in his life. "That sounds like a really good plan."

"That's what it's about, isn't it? Us being a team, watching each other's back."

She was absolutely right. "I can't believe I did this—that I almost blew it."

"Oh please," Caitie said. "It's going to take more than one stupid little argument to get rid of me."

He cupped her face in his hands. Kissed her. "I love you so much, Caitie."

She smiled and touched his face. "And I love you. It's always been you. And it always will be. So like it or not, you're stuck with me. For eternity."

He couldn't imagine a better way to spend forever. "We should go away for a few days. Take a trip together, just you, me and Cody."

"What did you have in mind?"

"I hear that New York is nice this time of year."

"But...I thought..."

"If it's important to you, then it's important to me, too. And you're right, Cody would have a blast."

"Are you sure?"

"I trust you."

"I'll call a travel agent."

Nate pulled her close and held her tight. He had planned to propose on a moonlit night, with flowers and soft music. And a ring. But he didn't want to wait another second. He pulled back, looked her in the eyes. "Marry me. Say you'll spend the rest of your life with me. I'll never be rich, not financially, but I promise that no one could ever love you as much as I do."

She smiled, touched his face again, pressed a gentle kiss to his lips and said, "I thought you'd never ask."

* * * * *

*If you liked this
Paradise, Colorado, story,
be sure to check out
Michelle Celmer's
NO ORDINARY JOE,
available as an ebook from
Harlequin Special Edition.*

#2311 ONCE UPON A VALENTINE
The Hunt for Cinderella • by Allison Leigh

Shea Weatherby isn't interested in love, but millionaire playboy Paxton Merrick has taken quite the human interest in this journalist's life story. When Shea finds herself pregnant after a passionate night with Pax, she must decide if she'll let down her guard for true love.

#2312 A SWEETHEART FOR JUDE FORTUNE
The Fortunes of Texas: Welcome to Horseback Hollow
by Cindy Kirk

Cupid hit cowboy Jude Fortune Jones right in the heart when he met Gabriella Mendoza. But the lovely Latina is hiding a secret—she's a heart transplant patient and might not be able to have children. Can the rancher romance his lady to a happily-ever-after?

#2313 THE REAL MR. RIGHT
Jersey Boys • by Karen Templeton

Single mom Kelly McNeil seeks refuge from her ex. In the process, she runs into her best friend's brother, hunky cop Matt Noble. Kelly and Matt forge a close bond, but she doesn't want to give up her newly found independence for him. Can Matt teach her how to love again?

#2314 REUNITING WITH THE RANCHER
Conard County: The Next Generation • by Rachel Lee

Returning to Conard County for her beloved aunt's funeral, social worker Holly Heflin can't avoid her ex, rancher Cliff Martin. Sparks ignite between them, but Holly is headed back to Chicago in two weeks. The city girl and the cowboy wonder if it's worth resurrecting the past to create a future....

#2315 CELEBRATION'S FAMILY
Celebrations, Inc. • by Nancy Robards Thompson

Widower Dr. Liam Thayer isn't looking for romance—least of all at a charity bachelor auction, where Kate Macintyre bids a hefty sum on the single dad. As Liam and Kate begin to fall in love, she begins to wonder whether she can ever truly be a part of his family.

#2316 THE DOCTOR'S FORMER FIANCÉE
The Doctors MacDowell • by Caro Carson

According to Dr. Lana Donnoli, her ex-fiancé, biotech millionaire Braden MacDowell, prefers profits over patients. When Braden returns home, he and Lana are thrown together over an accident, where they find that the past doesn't always stay there...and this time, "fiancée" might turn into "forever."

REQUEST YOUR FREE BOOKS!

2 FREE NOVELS PLUS 2 FREE GIFTS!

⊞ HARLEQUIN®

SPECIAL EDITION

Life, Love & Family

HSEI3R

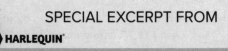
Jaded journalist Shea Weatherby isn't interested in romance—least of all, with a man like millionaire playboy Paxton Merrick. Shea falls pregnant after a passionate night with Pax, but she can create a real family with a bad-boy bachelor?

***

"You've got more experience to put on your resume now. If you really want to leave, do it."

She made a soft sound. "Probably not the best time for job hopping."

"Being pregnant, you mean." His soft words brushed against her temple and his thighs moved slowly against hers.

She exhaled shakily. "Mmm-hmm."

"You wouldn't have to work at all if you didn't want to."

She shook her head, though rubbing her cheek against the warmth radiating from him was probably the real motive. She forced herself to stop. To lift her head so there was at least one part of her not plastered against him.

She realized he'd danced her farther away from the others than she realized. "I'm not going to be your kept woman, Pax, if that's where you're heading."

His head lowered and she felt his lips against her cheek. "Baby mama doesn't fly for you?"

She slowly shook her head.

"What about wife?"

Something inside her chest fisted.

Beatrice had warned her he'd head that direction.

She pulled back again as far as his arm surrounding her would allow, which wasn't far. "Getting married just because I'm pregnant is a bad idea. We already agreed."

"I didn't agree," he said quietly. "I just didn't choose to debate the issue with you."

She didn't know why she was tearful all of a sudden. Only that she was, and there was no way he could fail to notice. "Please don't do this here," she whispered thickly.

He lifted one hand, touching her cheek gently. "Shea."

Tenderness from him would be her undoing. "You're supposed to be celebrating your best friend's wedding," she reminded.

"I'm celebrating my best friend's *marriage*. Anyone can have a wedding. Erik and Rory are going to have something a lot more important. Something that lasts a lifetime."

"And maybe they'll get there," she conceded huskily. "Right now they love each other, at least. They're starting out with a better reason than pregnancy."

His feet stopped moving altogether, though he still held her close. "Why is it so hard for you to see what's right in front of your face?"

Her throat felt like a vise was tightening around it. "I don't want us to end up hating each other."

Despite the dim lighting, his eyes searched hers, leaving her feeling raw. Exposed.

"There's no rule that says we will."

***

Enjoy this sneak peek from
USA TODAY *bestselling author Allison Leigh's*
ONCE UPON A VALENTINE, the latest book in
THE HUNT FOR CINDERELLA *miniseries.*

HSEEXPO114